IN THE FERTILE LAND

Also by Gabriel Josipovici

FICTION

The Inventory (1968)
Words (1971)
Mobius the Stripper: stories and short plays (1974)
The Present (1975)
Four Stories (1977)
Migrations (1977)
The Echo Chamber (1979)
The Air We Breathe (1981)
Conversations in Another Room (1984)
Contre-Jour: a triptych after Pierre Bonnard (1986)

THEATRE

Mobius the Stripper (1974)
Vergil Dying (1977)

NON-FICTION

The World and the Book (1971; 1979)
The Lessons of Modernism (1977; 1987)
Writing and the Body (1982)
The Mirror of Criticism: selected reviews (1983)
(ed.) The Modern English Novel: the reader, the
              writer and the book (1975)
(ed.) Selected Essays of Maurice Blanchot (1980)

GABRIEL JOSIPOVICI

IN THE FERTILE LAND

CARCANET

Acknowledgements

Grateful acknowledgement is made to the following publications where the stories first appeared: Arts Council Short Story Anthologies Nos 1 and 5, 'Second Person Looking Out' and 'Memories of a Mirrored Room in Hamburg'; *Nouvelle Revue Française* (in French translation) and *The Jewish Quarterly*, 'Brothers'; *Jewish Perspectives: Twenty-Five Years of Jewish Writing*, ed. Jacob Sonntag, 1980, 'Absence and Echo'; *Stand*, 'Children's Voices'; *Shakespeare Stories*, ed. Giles Gordon, 1982, 'A Changeable Report'; *Quarto*, 'Waiting'; *PN Review*, 'In the Fertile Land'; *The London Review of Books*, 'That Which is Hidden . . .' and 'Steps'; *Comparative Criticism*, ed. Elinor Shaffer, 1984, 'Vol. IV, pp. 167–9' and 'Exile'; *Four Stories*, 1977, 'He'; *Twenty Stories*, ed. Francis King, 1985, 'The Bitter End'. 'Death of the Word', 'The Bird Cage', 'Getting Better' and 'The Bitter End' were first read on BBC Radio 3.

First published in 1987 by
Carcanet Press Limited
208–212 Corn Exchange Buildings
Manchester M4 3BQ

and 198 Sixth Avenue
New York, New York 10013

British Library Cataloguing in Publication Data

Josipovici, Gabriel
  In the fertile land.
  1. Title
  823'.914 [F]   PR6060.064

  ISBN 0-85635-716-2

The publisher acknowledges the financial
assistance of the Arts Council of Great Britain

Typeset in Bembo by Paragon Photoset, Aylesbury
Printed in England by SRP Ltd, Exeter

Contents

Death of the Word

YESTERDAY I talked to my father. He stood in my room with his back to the window, facing the bed, his legs slightly apart, his hands behind his back, in the familiar posture. He has been dead for ten years.

We used to play ball when I was young, my father and I, Not football or cricket or any other known ball game, but simply 'ball'. 'Let's play ball,' my father would say, taking the beach-ball out of the cupboard under the stairs where we kept everything that didn't fit in anywhere else, and we would go out into the yard and begin the game. It started as a simple matter of throwing the ball to each other, backwards and forwards, but soon developed complex and rigid rules of its own, growing more and more violent until I would grab the ball and head for the park with it under my arm and him in hot pursuit. I remember my terror and exhilaration as I ran through the trees, hearing my father's footsteps in the grass behind me and feeling his hot breath on my neck. But nothing else. I remember nothing else. Whether he always caught me or always let me escape has vanished from my memory as completely as though we had never played at all. It is true that sometimes nowadays, while running for the bus or glancing idly out of a train window, I suddenly feel that this last part of the game is about to come back to me, but it never does. Is it that by becoming conscious of its imminent appearance I had somehow chased it away, or do I perhaps grow conscious of its presence before it has quite emerged precisely in order to prevent it from appearing? Whatever the reason, the conclusion of our ball game is lost to me, though I cannot think it can have been particularly traumatic, since we played almost every day and I was a singularly happy and untormented child.

Although my mother later told me that she admired my father greatly for his willingness to spend so much of his time with me, taking part in childish games, I think he enjoyed it even more than I did, and that having a child provided him with a wonderful excuse to indulge in such games with a clear conscience. I sensed this, even at the time, and he too seemed to realize that I saw through his elaborate game of double bluff, pretending to enjoy himself for my sake but actually enjoying it all thoroughly himself. So that we were accomplices in this, against my mother, and, having seen through his secret, I even held him to some extent in my power. Not that I could have acted on this power in any way, for it was intangible, a feeling, a sensation, but it was none the less true that whenever my father said, 'Let's play ball,' he put himself, so to speak, in my hands. And it was this, now I come to think of it, which really formed the mainspring of our game. The ball was only an excuse, a way of controlling and articulating this new and peculiar relationship between us. So that when I picked it up and tucked it under my arm and ran for the trees, I knew deep down inside me that if he caught me he would kill me for what I knew. And I must have known too that, however hard I tried to run, he would inevitably catch and kill me, annihilate me totally so that his secret should remain hidden for ever. And this I now see was what lent the ball-game its ambiguous mixture of pleasure and terror, for is it not what we all most deeply long for and also what we fear above all else, to be annihilated by the father who begot us?

My father was a big man. When he stood in front of the window he blotted out the light. In my memory he leans over me at a dangerous angle, like the Tower of Pisa, and I can chart my growth by his progressive return to the vertical, paralleled by the progressive diminution of his size. In fact I soon overtook him, and by the age of eighteen was able, if not to look down on him, at least to look squarely into his pale blue eyes and know that he would not be able to avoid me. Not that he ever wanted to. We were always having heart-to-heart talks at that time, and he would gaze intensely at me, coming into my room late at night and standing between my desk and the bed, blotting out the light. He was a great believer in heart-to-heart talks, and would hold forth for hours about his own youth in the mountains and his relations with his own father. I never answered him when he started off on this tack, preferring to lie with my hands under my head and look at the halo of light surrounding him. But my silence seemed to spur him to greater and greater feats of reminiscence and description, and he would end by glancing at his watch and clearing his throat, coming forward and patting me on the head, saying: 'I'm glad we understand each other so well.' I felt then and still feel that he wanted to talk to me about something but could never quite bring himself to do so, hoping that I would ask or that his endless fund of stories would lead naturally in that direction. But since he was half aware of the problem himself there could be no question of its coming up naturally, and as I never asked he never revealed to me what it was. I think he realized at moments that I was aware of something and deliberately avoided asking, and he tried to manoeuvre me into it; but he held the weaker hand and we remained as we were. I have often wondered what it was that nagged him like that and whether he would have become a different man had I allowed him to bring it out into the open, but idly, and without really looking for an answer. Certainly it was no 'thing' – guilty secret or other banal fact – which could have been taken out and exhibited or in any way dealt with by positive action. But there was undoubtedly a core of anxiety there, and had he managed to talk to me about it it would no doubt have ceased to trouble him so much – but then he would have had to be a different person and so would I and the whole question would not have arisen.

I had a letter the other day from a girl I proposed to ten years ago and who turned me down, saying that she often asked herself whether our marriage would have worked and whether we would have been happy. But what does 'we' mean in such a context? We are made by our choices. The people we are today are so different from the people we would have been had we in fact got married that the question is entirely without meaning. We are not one self but many, held together by the memories of a common past registered on our single body. That is the pathos of memory and of the sentimentality it engenders, which is the belief that one can have choice without renunciation, that one can be both what one is and what one might have been. Clearly what I am today was shaped by the girl's refusal. And yet how much of *me* was there even behind the question I put to her? I wonder.

My father was incurably sentimental. I think I felt this from quite early on. I was repelled by his constant attempts to hold on to the moment and replay it to himself as it were, with me as the necessary audience. It frightened me, especially – perhaps only – because he was my father. After all, he was there before me. He will loom over me, between my bed and the light, for the rest of my life.

Indeed, it is difficult to see how it could be otherwise. We cannot imagine that what has been there when we arrive will one day cease to exist. It has about it the permanence of the unquestionable. For our parents to die is as unthinkable as that the world should one day disappear. That is why the death of a father is the traumatic event of a lifetime. It pushed Freud into writing *The Interpretation of Dreams*, and one wonders how Kafka's work would have altered if his father had preceded him to the grave. Mourning and melancholia, Freud said, are our two ways of responding to this catastrophic event, but that is perhaps to see the matter in too crude a light (though it must be said in fairness that Freud was as well aware of this as anyone). We are never really in doubt about our own mortality, though we try to suppress the knowledge of it as much as possible, hoping against hope that a miracle will occur and that we, of all the multitudes who have existed since the creation of the world, will prove immortal. Far worse, because so totally unthinkable, is the fact of a father's death. We use thought to protect ourselves from pain; what cannot be thought pierces us where we are weakest and we succumb.

I remember the day my father died. It was the middle of winter. The trees were bare. The snow had come and gone and come again and was now melting in black puddles on the edges of the pavements. My mother rang me up, telling me to come at once, and I put down the phone and walked straight out of the house and up to the station. I don't know how long I waited for the train or how long the train took to get there, but when I arrived he was dead. When I arrived he was dead.

He had a way of lying in bed with his feet sticking up through the blankets which my eldest son also favours. In many ways they are alike, and in my son I seem to see my father, as though they were one and the same person and had no use for me, holding them apart, but would crush me between them and regain their lost unity. It is normal, I believe, for fathers to see themselves in their sons – their youthful selves, hopes unblighted, the world before them. But this is only another instance of sentimentality and I will have no truck with it.

I remember walking with my son along an alley-way lined with trees. It was autumn and the leaves were thick on the ground. It had been a dry summer and they were yellower than honey. My son waved his arms as he talked, driving home his points, each with a gesture, and I thought suddenly that I would always be in the position of listening and watching while others drove home their points. When I wake up nowadays I often have the feeling that we have just emerged from that long alley-way with the autumn trees and the thick carpet of leaves, and that it is impossible for us to turn round and walk slowly back the other way.

The other day I woke up like that, with the sense of that tree-lined alley-way still vivid in my mind and body. It was night. In the distance I heard lorries rumbling through the city. The street-light shone brightly outside the window and patterned the ceiling with unreal colours. The house was silent though someone coughed overhead. It is odd that there are no books on the classification of coughs heard in the night. They are so many and so varied. The unreal sounds of a buried world. I sat at the window and watched the empty street, while the sky changed from yellow to pink and then to streaky blue. When the light in the street went out I returned to bed, careful to make no sound for the springs creak dreadfully and I do not like to advertise my presence to all and sundry.

I was looking out of the kitchen window the day my father died. It was the middle of winter. The trees were bare. The snow had come and gone and come again and was now melting in black puddles on the edges of the pavements. I had switched on the electric kettle to make some coffee and was looking out of the window at the white sky when the phone rang. I went out into the hall and picked up the receiver, leaving the door open so that I could go on looking at the sky. When I heard what my mother had to say I put down the receiver and walked straight out of the house and to the station, forgetting about the kettle. Nothing fused but the kettle was ruined.

The trees were bare. The snow had come and gone. When I got there he was dead. They had thrown a sheet over him and he lay there as he used to do on Sundays, with his feet sticking up through the blankets in a way my son also favours. In many ways they are alike, my father and my eldest son.

I remember walking with my son along an alley-way lined with trees. It was autumn and the leaves were thick on the ground. It had been a dry summer.

It had been a dry summer. I remember thinking

But why should I go on? Where have they come from, these winters and summers, these autumns and springs, these white skies and yellow skies and streaky blue skies, these gesticulating sons and honey leaves? They have nothing to do with me or with my father.

I sit in my room. Other people move about. Doors open and close as they go off to work. Fortunately I am spared the necessity of doing so myself. I make some tea and tidy the bed. Then I sit in the armchair and look out of the window and think about my father.

Yesterday I talked to my father. He stood in my room with his back to the window, facing the bed, in the familiar posture. He has been dead for ten years. I remember the day he

I remember nothing. No wife. No sons. No autumn days or ruined kettles. And then it must be said: no room either, with bed and chair, banging doors or coughing neighbours. I sit at my desk and write: Yesterday I talked to my father. And then I have to admit: no father either. Oh I must have had one once, but not that kind, not that kind. No ball-game. No heart to heart talks. No secret complicity. No phone call. No death.

But now I have said that I begin to understand. I see that I do after all have a father. He is the first sentence I wrote down: Yesterday I talked to my father. Before today there was yesterday. Before that, another day. Before the first word, another word, making the first one possible. Without that, without my father, a time before, there could be no present, no future. I would suffocate.

My father is the phrase that begins it all and also that against which it is all directed. For now it is clear to me that these so-called memories which have come to me in the wake of that initial sentence have had only one purpose: to oust my father from his pre-eminent position, to annihilate him, to remove him forever from his place between myself and the light.

He was there: framed in the window, black upon white. But now I have succeeded in removing him, first by casting doubt upon his motives, then by casting doubt upon his existence, I find it difficult to go on. Without my father, against whom to push, I cannot continue. If there is no room, no bed, no chair no father blotting out the light, then what am I and where am I? I am only this sentence, hesitating, uncertain, with nowhere to go and nothing to say any more. It is as though the assassination of my father had started my own slow death, since even saying I am this sentence means nothing any more, now that the pretext has gone, body blotting out the light, standing between me and the window, and all that is left is pure light, white page at last, waiting with infinite patience as the sentence vacillates, falters, and I gather myself for one last hopeless cry: Father, father, why have you forsaken me?

Second Person Looking Out

I

'IN the house,' says my guide, 'there are seventeen rooms. And each room has three windows, which can be moved to any position of the walls or covered over if necessary.'

'Is it a temple?' I ask, hurrying to keep up with him. Although he does not appear to walk fast his pace is deceptive.

'No no,' my guide says. 'A private house.'

The path is narrow and winds round hillocks and down into little valleys before plunging again into thick woods. My guide does not wait for me or make any concessions to my lack of experience of the terrain. He moves forward without effort, throwing the words back over his left shoulder.

'If you go from one room to another,' he says, 'the head of the house, your host, may move a window fractionally along the wall or transplant it to another wall altogether, so that when you return to the first room you see another landscape outside, differently framed.'

Inside the house people stand in tight groups, drinking champagne out of long-stemmed glasses and talking loudly. I stand at the window, looking out.

'What you experience as you approach the house,' my guide says, 'is very important. First you may see a little bit of the house, then it disappears for several minutes, then you see another aspect of it, because the path is winding gradually round it. And when you finally reach it, because you are constantly seeing fragments of it and imagining it when you can't see it, you've experienced it in a million forms, you've already lived in the house, whole dramas have occurred before you even reach it, centuries have elapsed and you are still as far away from it as ever.'

The path is narrow, so that it is impossible for the two of us to walk abreast. At times I have to break into a run to keep up with him.

'How far is it still?' I ask him.

'We will soon be there,' he says.

We trudge on through the thick trees. The sky is invisible from here and it is impossible to tell the time of day. My guide has explained to me: 'When you leave the house many of the paths will be barred to you. A small bamboo stick will be placed across the entrance, some fifty metres down the path. Do not try to cross the bamboo sticks. Retrace your steps. Follow the stones which have a piece of string tied round them and fastened in a triple knot.'

'Excuse me,' someone says. It is a white-coated waiter with a tray of long-stemmed glasses filled to the brim with sparkling champagne. I take a glass from the tray.

'The house,' my guide says.

I look through the trees but can see only hills beyond and then more trees beyond that.

'Where?' I ask him.

'We can no longer see it,' he says. 'Please pay attention and look at once when I tell you.'

He is a small stocky man with an even pace. He walks without stopping or looking back at me.

As we come round the edge of a hillock I see a light in the distance. 'Is that it?' I ask him.

He hurries on ahead of me.

'Is that the house?' I ask again.

'That is the house.'

'When do we get there?' I ask him. 'How far is it now?'

The house has disappeared again. We are walking across open heathland. The sky is quite blue overhead.

'The heath you see over there,' the waiter says, pointing with his chin, 'that is where they will come from.'

'Who?' I ask him.

He turns away. I stretch out my hand and take a glass from his tray. I wander into another room.

I have been in this room before, but the windows have been moved. Now, instead of three windows on the one wall, all looking out over the same prospect, there is only one on that side and two on the wall opposite.

'It is a habit of the house,' my host explains, showing me round. 'The windows are moved once a guest has looked through them.'

'That must be disconcerting for the guest,' I say, laughing.

'It is the habit,' he says.

He stands beside me, looking out over the darkening landscape. 'A guide is given for the return journey,' he says. 'Never for the journey here.'

'I came with a guide,' I say.

'For the return journey,' he repeats.

'But I came with a guide,' I say. 'He told me about the house. The windows.'

'In that case,' he says, 'it was the return journey.'

People are pressing into us on all sides, talking and laughing. My host says: 'To find your way out you follow the stones that have a piece of string tied round them and fastened with a triple knot.'

I am in another room. My host has gone. I stand, looking out of the window.

Suddenly my guide says: 'Over there.' I look up quickly and true enough, the house is visible once more, very close now, though still somewhat masked by the trees.

'We must be almost there,' I say.

But the path must wind away from the house because the next time it appears it seems to be a good deal further off.

'But when do we arrive?' I ask my guide.

'We have arrived,' he says.

'No no,' I say. 'I mean at the house itself. Not just the grounds.'

'The distinction is meaningless,' he says, hurrying forward.

The waiter returns with his tray of champagne. My host takes one of the glasses and hands it to me. He himself already has a half-empty glass in his hand.

'Welcome!' he says.

'Why do you welcome me now,' I say, 'when we have already been talking for some time?'

He shrugs. 'It is the custom,' he says.

I turn back to the window, but it has disappeared.

'It is done with screens,' my host explains. 'Paper screens.'

He adds: 'Shall we move into the next room? There are people there I would like you to meet.'

II

He has walked through the seventeen rooms. He has talked to many of the guests as well as to his host. At times he has stopped alone in front of a window and stared out at the landscape.

It has been explained to him that the house is approached by numerous paths. Some of them, he has been told, will be closed when he leaves, but, by following those stones which have a piece of string tied round them and fastened in a triple knot he will be able to find his way out.

'How much further is it?' he asks his guide.

'Not much further,' the man says, hurrying ahead.

They round a hillock and there is the house ahead of them.

'There are seventeen rooms in the house,' the guide explains. 'Each room has three windows, which can be moved to any position on the walls or covered over if necessary.'

His host has moved away from him and wandered into the next room. The young lady to whom he has just been introduced asks him: 'Is this a temple or something?'

'No. Just a private house.'

'It reminds me of a temple,' she says.

They are standing in the fourteenth room. The three windows all face the tall trees at the back of the house. The light from the downstairs rooms illuminates the lawn, but that only serves to make it darker under the trees. His host, in answer to a question, explains: 'The windows are always moved once a guest has looked through them.'

'That must be disconcerting for the guest,' he says.

'It is the custom,' his host says, standing beside him in the darkness.

He advances slowly, feeling each step ahead of him for fear of treading on a bamboo stick laid across the path. Every now and again he lights a match and holds it close to the ground, looking for the stones which have a piece of string tied round them and fastened in a triple knot.

'Do temples have to be holy?' the girl asks him. 'I mean,' she adds laughing, 'couldn't people be having a party in a temple?'

There are too many people in each room. They stand, wedged together, holding their long-stemmed glasses and talking. There is nowhere to sit down.

'I mean,' the girl says, 'it would be original, wouldn't it, a party in a temple?'

His guide moves with even steps, always ahead. He throws comments and instructions over his left shoulder, for the path is too narrow for two people to walk abreast. 'Don't lag,' he says. 'Look when I point.'

The rooms are packed with people. He pushes his way through, muttering apologies, looking for his host. Eventually he finds him, on his own, by a window, looking out.

'It is time for me to leave,' he says, bowing slightly and bringing his hands together in front of his chest.

His host shrugs, but does not answer.

'I have been into all the rooms,' he says, 'and looked through all the windows. I have talked to all the guests.'

'There are always new guests,' his host says smiling. 'And new positions for the windows.'

'Nevertheless, it is time for me to leave.'

'Patience,' his host says. 'Patience. Follow the stones which have a piece of string tied round them and you cannot go wrong.'

'Yes,' he says. 'I will do that. Don't worry about me.'

'You have tried seventeen paths,' his host says. 'Perhaps the eighteenth will not be blocked.'

They resume their slow progress under the dark trees.

'I am surprised you cannot direct me to the right path,' he says, stopping in the darkness.

His host laughs. 'I can only counsel you,' he says. 'You would not want me to make your decisions for you, would you?' He adds: 'But it is highly unlikely that there are many more than eighteen paths.'

They move forward again and a light comes into view, high up through the trees. It is a window of the house. Inside, the party still seems to be in progress. People crowd the room and a waiter in a white jacket circulates with a tray of long-stemmed glasses. A man stands alone at the window, looking out.

'Why eighteen?' he asks.

His host laughs again in the darkness beside him. 'I don't know,' he says. 'Eighteen seems to be a realistic number.'

They start to walk down the eighteenth path.

'Goodbye,' his host says, bowing formally from the waist and starting to back into another room. 'Thank you for coming.' He adds: 'A servant will show you to the door.'

III

You walk alone under the trees. You seek the path that will lead you out.

You follow the stones with the string tied round them and fastened in a triple knot. When a bamboo stick is laid across the path you turn back and start again.

You know that by now you should be almost within reach of the house.

You move quickly from room to room, looking for your host.

You touch the stones, feeling in the darkness for the string.

'It is a private house,' your guide says. 'Inside, a party is in progress. People stand in tight groups in each of the rooms, sipping champagne and talking loudly. One or two stand at windows, looking out.'

'That is the way you go when you leave,' the girl to whom you have just been introduced explains to you. Her husband, it turns out, is in the diplomatic service. You have already had a long talk with her, but in another room.

You start along another path, having retraced your steps again upon encountering the thin bamboo stick laid neatly across the track.

'In a moment we will be there,' your guide says.

You ask your host if the house has always belonged to his family.

'Good heavens no!' he says. 'I wish it had,' he adds, and laughs.

Fifteen stones with string tied round them and fastened in a triple knot have followed each other in rapid succession. The path has grown broader. You light a match and hold it down close to the ground. Another stone comes into view. The string tied neatly round it gives it the appearance of a parcel waiting to be picked up.

You turn round to see how far you have come, but the path must have curved without your noticing and neither the house nor any of its lighted windows is anywhere to be seen.

'Should we not have arrived by now?' you ask your guide.

'Keep on your toes,' he says, and you are not sure if you are meant to take this literally or if he is simply using an expression he has picked up. 'When I give the word,' he says, 'look up at once.'

You look up. But where a moment before there was a window there is now only a blank wall.

'Don't be surprised,' your host says. 'Even seventeen stones with string tied round them and fastened in a triple knot do not necessarily imply an eighteenth.'

'No,' you say. 'I suppose not.' You move your foot forward with care, feeling for the bamboo stick.

And sure enough the stick is there. Now that the position of the window has been altered you can just make it out, gleaming whitely under the trees at the turn in the path.

Memories of a Mirrored Room in Hamburg

– There was no war, he says. There were no trenches. There
was no mud.

Six times mirrored in the room: a round, glass-topped
table; a vase; a single lily; a bottle; two glasses; a chair; a man in
uniform without his cap; a naked woman on his knee.

He says: – There was no war. There was no mud. I did not
die.

In the mirrored walls, the mirrored floor, the mirrored
ceiling: a table; a vase; a bottle; a chair; a man in uniform and a
naked woman on his knee.

– Prosit! she says, and raises her glass.

– There was no mud, he says. There was no gas. I did not
die. I am not dead.

– To the future, she says, and drinks.

He laughs.

Her arms round his neck. Six times mirrored.

– Tell, she says. Tell me more. Tell me a little more.

– There was no, he says. I did not.

The opening. The opening of her body. In the floor. The
ceiling.

– Tell, she says. Tell me. Her arm round his neck. Tell. Her
hand on his flies.

His head thrown back. Her hand.

Her arms round my

Sagging body on my

The table. The two glasses. The bottle. The vase. The
flower.

Her hands at his back, caressing.

– Tell, she says. Tell about the.

He says: – There was no gas. There were no shells. I did not die.

Flesh on my
How did I
– Prosit! she says. They drink, heads thrown back. Reflected are: the table, the vase, the flower, the bottle, the man, the woman, heads thrown back, drinking.

– Now, he says.
– No, she says.
– Now, he says.
– No, she says. Tell me more. Tell me more.

Kiss. They kiss. – Tell, she says. In his mouth, she says. To the future.

The opening. The opening of her body reflected in the floor. The floor in the ceiling. – Tell, she says. Her hand on his flies.

His head thrown back. Her hand on his flies.
– There was no war, he says. I did not.

The table. The bottle. The two glasses. The vase. The flower. The man in his uniform. The naked woman.

– Now, he says.
– No, she says. Not yet.
– Now, he says. Now.

She raises her glass. Tosses her red hair – Again the future. He laughs. She says: – Tell. Tell me you must tell.

– Now, he says. Now. It must.
– No, she says, mouth on his. Tell about the. Tell about the. Tell about the mud.

– There was no mud, he says. There was no war. There was no gas.

The room. Six times reflected are: the table, the vase, the flower, the bottle, the two glasses, the chair, the man, the woman, nothing else in the mirrored room.

He says: – There was no mud. There were no trenches. I am not dead.

Her arms round my
Flesh on my

Raise her glass and
Round my neck her lips on
– Tell, she says. Tell me more. Her hand in. Head back.
Mouth open.
    – Tell me, she says.
    – There was no.
    – No what?
    – There was no.
    – No?
    – Now, he says. It must.
    – No, she says. Not yet, she says.
    – Yes, he says. Now.
    – Tell, she says. Tell about the.
    – I am not. I was not.
On the floor savagely I
Arms round my face back in my
    – Prosit! she says, and tips back the glass.
On the floor and her above lapping up and lapping up how
did I come where is it where is it now I come I
    – The future! she says, and raises her glass. Seven times
raises her glass in the empty room.
On the floor and where I
Seven times her arms round his neck vase on the table her
sagging weight on his knee they kiss they kiss.
    Coming now rolling on the glass the floor the glass she
laughs head back mouth open how did I come here where is
the exit where is the where.
    Laughs, holding out her glass, tossing her hair, he refills,
she says: – Tell. Tell.
    – I did not. There was no.
Where is the exit where
Raises her glass and toasts the future the end of the end of
the end of the
    Coming now rolling glass floor cold smooth reflect the
rolling over and over where are you now where are you now
where
    I was not there. I did not fight. I did not.

– I, she says, rolling. I fight, I, rolling, over and over now on top now below, I, she says, I fight, she says, I fight for I fight for I fight for I

The table. The vase. The flower. The bottle. The two glasses. The chair. The man in uniform. The naked red-haired woman on his knee.

– Warm me, she says. Warm me warm me warm me warm me.

Faster rolling faster into the table the vase crashing bottle breaking her back red with blood I

– Prosit! she says, tips back her glass, red hair tossing.

I drink I lick I come I

– Now! she says. Yes now! she says.

There was no mud. I did not. I am not.

– Yes now! she says. Yes now yes now yes now yes now yes.

Rolling and rolling now he says now he says quick he says I he says now he says now

The table. The chair. The vase. The flower. The bottle. The man in uniform. The naked woman on his knee. They raise their glasses.

He says: – There was no war. There were no trenches. There was no mud. I did not die.

The mirrored room. In the ceiling, the floor, the four walls: a table, a vase, a single flower, a bottle, two glasses, a chair, a man in uniform, without his cap, a naked woman on his knee.

– There was no war, he says. I did not die. I am not dead.

Did not. Am not.

Did not. Am not.

– Yes, he says. There was no war. There was no mud. I did not die. I am not. I am not dead.

Brothers

HE climbs the stairs. I know him by his tread. My brother!
The door creaks a little as he pushes it. Now he steps inside
and says hello. He stands by the door and looks round. What a
funny place to be, he says. Not the house, he adds. The house
is very nice. Very nice indeed. But why do you sit here in the
dusk like that? I knew it was you, I tell him. He comes
forward into the room. There is nowhere for him to sit. There
is only the table in the middle of the room, with its chair, and
I am already sitting on the chair. He walks to the window and
leans against the sill. I knew it was you, I tell him. I know your
tread. I called, he says. I knocked. I only let myself in when no
one answered. I tell him I heard someone call, but it seemed a
long way off, and then there was silence, broken only by a dog
barking in the distance. He repeats what a nice house it is and
how well I have done for myself and how quiet and secluded it
is. I almost could not get through because of the snow, he
says. He asks me to return with him, he asks me to cease to
turn my head away from things and come back. I explain to
him that back has no meaning for me. He insists that it is
nothing to do with my wife, that that is entirely my own
affair, that he has come of his own accord, that he cannot let
me do this to myself. It upsets him that I do not respond to
this. I tell him about the snow. I tell him how I wake up
thinking I am lying in the snow, a black figure on the white
hillside, and I have just been dreaming that I am in my clean
and empty room at the top of the house and have received of
all things a visit from my brother. I am lying in the snow and
yet I can still feel myself in the room, deep in conversation
with my brother. The ties between us are so close that it is not

a matter of what we say at all. He does not want me to break free as I have done, it makes him feel imprisoned in the web of his own commitments. But also it makes him feel anxious for my sake, more anxious than he would be for his own. The two things, the envy and the concern, cannot be disentangled, either on his side or on mine. When I tell him about the snow and the cold hillside in the dawn he grows angry, waves his arms, tells me not to be silly. I ask him if he is not ever prone to such imaginings himself, if driving down in his car for instance he did not at moments think himself in my place, even perhaps imagine himself lying in the snow, inert, with a dog barking at this black unmoving shape, and if it was not perhaps something of a relief to feel that it was all over, at last. He does not answer. He looks out of the window, at the woods and the hills beyond and the snow on the hills. He repeats that enough is enough, that I have made my point and now I should come back. I never thought you would do it, he says, you talked about it so much. He assures me he has not come as an emissary from my wife, though she does of course need me and would welcome me back, as would the children. He tells me it is entirely on his own initiative that he has come, that he drove down in the early hours, when all of London was still asleep, and kept on driving until he reached me. Now he has come to take me back. I am not sure that this is what he has really come for. I wonder if it is not to talk about himself, to ask my advice, to tell me that he needs my help in order to escape from the life that has trapped him. You turn your head away, he says. You refuse to listen. I tell him that I am glad he is here, that in some obscure way I had been waiting for his tread on the stair, that I have often, since I have come here, imagined this scene between us in the long, clean, low-ceilinged room, that it is as if we had always been here, together, talking. He interrupts me to say that I always turn the specific into the general, that I dissolve one thing into another and so evade decisions. He repeats that I must return with him, that I cannot do what I have done. I know that he is waiting for me to persuade him, that it would disappoint him deeply were I to accede to his request and return with him, though in another way of course it would please him, it would show him that he was the stronger and more decisive of us two.

And of course he is also genuinely concerned about me, he is worried to see me alone, sitting at a table in the dusk in the middle of an empty room, at the top of an empty house, doing nothing. I could of course return with him, merely to show myself that I am strong enough for anything, that I am not cowering here out of weakness. Yet to do so would be a show of weakness rather than of strength. I really have no need of him. I have my house and my table and my chair and I have turned my head from all the rest, as he so rightly observes, so there is an end to it. He has perched himself on the sill of the window in a rather awkward way, and now waits for me to reply. I tell him about my walks in the snow. I tell him how as I sit here at the table in the middle of an empty room I sometimes feel with absolute clarity that I am lying in the snow, one hand flung out, the other over my heart. A dog barks nearby, barks at this prostrate form, but I do not move. The dog's bark grows more and more distant. I am lying in the snow but at the same time I am sitting in my quiet room in the dusk, and I hear the tread of my brother's footsteps on the stairs. I wait for him to enter. He pushes the door open a little and it creaks as he does so, then he is inside the room and we are talking as we have always talked. I ask him if he is not subject to such fantasies. He turns his back to me and looks out of the window. He wants me to cease this nonsense. He wants me to return to my family, my home, my job. He wants me to stay here, is proud of me for doing what I have done. So it has always been between us. He drives his little car along the motorway with the snow piled up on either side and in his mind's eye he can see me sitting in the dusk at my table in the middle of the empty room, he can see me lying on the hillside, a dark figure, one hand flung out and the other over his heart. He approaches and bends over me. His legs are stiff from all the driving he has had to do that day. He looks into my face, and as he does so he realizes it is himself he is looking at. That is what our lives have always been like, entangled one with the other to the point sometimes of total confusion. That is why we have got on so badly. As he drives he is lying out on the hillside, his body is growing cold. A dog has seen the prostrate form and barks in a fury of anxiety. I have died in peace, he thinks, my brother at least did not try to pester me, did not attempt to pull me back. He did not drive down in his little car and try to persuade me to return. Perhaps there is, for a moment, just a hint of resentment at his brother for not doing so, a feeling, fleetingly experienced, that if he is now dying like this in the snow it is his brother's fault for making no move to save him from himself. But that is quickly dissipated in the larger sense of peace. For his brother has come, after all, there is his tread on the stair. I sit in my room, he thinks, and there is my brother, after all. My heart fills with joy. He has come! In a minute he will be in the room with me. He has driven all the way down from London, setting out when it was still dark and driving for hours through the snow-covered countryside. Now he is here, with me, talking. It does not matter what we say to each other. It is only important that he is here. He checks to see how many miles he has done since he left the house and returns to imagining what it will be like when he arrives. Perhaps this time too, he thinks, I will know how I really feel towards him. Perhaps I will suddenly understand if it is pity or envy I feel towards him. The dog barks but now there is no one to hear it. It draws near to the prostrate form and sniffs, then utters a howl and backs away. My brother turns from the window. Please, he says. It is I who need you. When he says that my heart warms towards him. It does not matter what words pass between us. What matters is that he is here, with me, in the big, low-ceilinged room, and that we are talking.

The Bird Cage

SO you are in the house at last. How well you describe the room. The sea. The window. The bird in the cage. The mirror. And then in the mirror the cage, the window and the sea.

When I read what you say I long to be there, with you, in that room brimming with light and the sea and the bird.

You ask me to come. You describe the way the light fills the room. You describe the way the mirror reflects the light which bounces off the sea. You describe the way the song of the bird mingles with the sound of the waves. I can't wait. I can't wait to come.

I will catch the train this afternoon. In a few hours I will be there. Tomorrow morning I will wake and see the foot of the bed in the mirror and then the cage and the bird and the window and the sea. Last night I dreamed about the bird. About the yellowness of its plumage. You tell me about his song, the sound of his voice, and in my dream it is translated into colours, the colour of his plumage. I wish I knew what that meant. What that dream meant, the transposition in the dream.

I am here now and you are gone. I came and we were together and now you are gone.

I am glad you are not here. I am glad to be able to possess the room myself as you possessed it before I came. I am glad to be able to stand at the window and look into the sea and let the song of the bird fill me up entirely. I am glad to wake alone and look in the mirror and see the foot of the bed and the bird in his cage and the window and the sea outside. I am glad to be able to take possession of it as you took possession of it. In that way I feel I am getting to know you as well as I know myself.

I am glad you have had to go away. I am glad to be alone here with nothing but the sea and the gulls and the bird in the cage. I stand for hours under his cage, looking at the sea. The light reflected off the sea almost hurts. It makes everything in the room seem to splinter into a thousand fragments, as if it could not contain itself, there was so much light. I never draw the curtains. At night I feel myself going to sleep in the middle of the sea. When I wake in the morning I keep my eyes closed for a moment, feeling the light exploding in my body. That's what it does, it explodes in my body. I don't count the days. Sometimes I imagine I have not yet arrived and only have your descriptions to fire my imagination. Sometimes it is almost too much to bear in the present.

I am glad to be here by myself but I begin to miss you. I wonder why you have not yet returned, what it is that is keeping you so long. I have begun to think of how you looked those last few days. I have begun to wonder if you are ever coming back. Yesterday I walked to the farm with the intention of ringing you but when I got there I couldn't do it. Won't you write to me? Won't you tell me when you are coming back?

This morning I walked to the farm and asked to use the phone. I dialled your number but when I heard the phone ringing in your flat I put the instrument straight back. I think I couldn't face hearing the sound of you withdrawing when you learned who it was at the other end. Perhaps tomorrow I will have more courage, be able to go through with it.

I have decided to go away. I have decided that you will not come back here until I go away. I stand at the window and look at the sea and I know I will have to go away. I will bring the bird round to the farm when I bring them the key. Perhaps when you learn that I have gone away you will be able to return.

I had expected an explanation but you have provided none.

I had expected the phone to ring in my flat but it was silent. And now you write as though nothing had happened. You write about the bird and the room as you did before. Before I came. As if I had never been and you had never gone and left me there, for a day or two you said, while you dealt with urgent matters in town. What is the meaning of your letter?

You write and ask me to come, as though nothing had happened. I do not know what to make of what you write. You say you are selling the house and want me to see it for one last time. I cannot understand what it is you are asking.

You beg me to answer and let you know if I have received your letters. You tell me the house is sold with the bird and the bed and the mirror and everything else. You say you want to see me and beg me to answer. How can I answer a letter like that?

You write and tell me the owner has allowed the house to go to ruin. You write go to ruin as if that were the most natural thing in the world, and as if the English were correct. Perhaps it is but it feels wrong to me. I would have said fall into ruin, but perhaps it is I who am at fault. You write that you have been back and walked along the beach and pushed open the door because no one lives in the house any more and it is an adventure, to walk along the beach and see this lovely and deserted house right up against the sea which is not locked and climb the stairs which are rotting and enter the bedroom. You write that you would like to buy back the house and restore it. You write that the mirror still stands in the bedroom, reflecting the foot of the bed and the window and the sea. You write that the cage is still there but the bird has gone. I don't know why you write these things to me or what you want of me. You say you do not know if the bird is dead or the owner has found him a better cage. I don't know why you write like this. I remember the light in the room when we woke in the morning and the light of the evening when I stood by myself at the window but most of all I remember how I imagined the room when you first wrote to me about it.

How can I answer your letters? What do you want me to say? I showed my little girl the picture you had drawn, of the mirror and the room reflected in it, and, beyond the window, the sea. She said the bird was singing. I asked her how she knew but she giggled the way children do and wouldn't answer.

I don't think you understand. I don't think you have much idea what happens to us in our lives. I don't think you see that we are all in cages, but the cages are our lives. You wanted to build a cage around yourself and then you were afraid when you saw the bars. But there is no need to build. The cages are our lives. When we recognize this we can sing. That is what I think at least.

I say these words to myself: the sea, the window, the bird, the cage, the room, the mirror, and then the room again, the cage, the window and the sea. They are like the bars of my cage. My little girl asks me if I will ever take her to the room by the sea. I tell her: you are there. You are in the room. There is no need to go. She does not hear when I speak. She looks at the picture. The picture on the page. I say: Turn the page. Let us look at another picture. She does not hear. She is absorbed by what is in front of her, as children are. Turn the page, I say. Turn the page and let us look at another picture. But she does not hear.

Absence and Echo

On looking at Vermeer's A Young Woman Standing
at a Virginal *in the National Gallery, London.*

– Tell me. Tell me.
– What?
– What is she doing? What is she doing now?
– Standing.
– Just standing?
– She's looking round. Her hands are on the keyboard.
– She's playing?
– No. She has finished playing.
– Finished?
– For the moment. Or perhaps she is about to start.
– Why has she stopped?
– Like that.
– What do you mean like that?
– She just has.
– Oh.
– Perhaps she's listening.
– Listening?
– To the music fading. Or to a noise, a whisper, outside. Or
perhaps she's just turning. Looking in this direction.
– Is she alone?
– Yes.
– And she's still standing? Listening?
– Light enters from the window behind her. The room is
filled with light. Her hands rest on the keyboard.
– Can you see through the window?
– No. It is only the source of light.

– Go on.

– She waits. There is the trace of a smile on her lips. She turns towards us.

– She is smiling? At us?

– No.

– What else is there in the room?

– There are two paintings on the wall behind her. There is a chair between us and the keyboard.

– Describe the paintings.

– Near the window, in a golden frame, there is a small landscape. The sky is very blue.

– Go on.

– The other is behind and above her. It hangs exactly in the middle of the rear wall. Her head bisects the left hand bottom corner so that the ebony frame encloses her face as well as the picture.

– What is the subject?

– It is a Cupid. A naked boy holding a bow in his right hand, facing the room. In his left hand he holds aloft a card or little book.

– A card?

– It is impossible to be more precise.

– Is she aware of the Cupid?

– No. She turns her head away from it. She looks towards us.

– Us?

– Perhaps she is not smiling. But she is not sad either.

– What is her expression then?

– She is turning. The light catches the right side of her face, her neck. It rises off the chair, the wood of the instrument. Perhaps she is listening.

– Listening?

– To the music. To her memory of the music. Perhaps.

– What instrument is she playing?

– A virginal. It is delicately marbled. The strings are just visible. On the lid, which is laid back, a landscape is painted. She stands in front of the instrument, her back to the window.

– What is there outside the window?

– Nothing. It is the source of light, as I have said.

– And she has still not moved?

– She half turns. Her body faces the painted landscape on the lid of the instrument. Behind her, on the wall, the Cupid stands upright.

– Why is he there?

– He is an echo.

– An echo?

– Of the music. As the painted landscape is an echo of the trees and meadow outside the window.

– And us? She cannot hear us? She is not aware of our presence?

– Who knows? She listens. For a moment her body listens. To the fading of the music. To the light. To the picture behind her.

– She thinks about it?

– No. It echoes.

– Will she move away? Will she come towards us?

– No.

– Then what will she do?

– She does not belong to the world of doing. Though her body listens to the echoes of the upright Cupid.

– You mean she will do nothing? Even if she discovers us?

– She will not discover us. She does not belong to our time.

– But when the echoes are stilled? When she grows tired of standing?

– She belongs where she stands.

– She is not real then? She belongs to mythology?

– She is no nymph. We know who she is. But for a moment which lasts for ever she cannot see or hear us.

– Even if we intrude upon her? Will she not see us then? Not hear us?

– We cannot intrude upon her. She exists within the cube of light which is the room. We are outside.

– We cannot go in? We cannot call out to her?

– No.

– She exists outside time? Outside our time?

– She has made time her own. It no longer has power over her. She is time, Cupid and echo.

– And we? What are we?

– We are divided where she is single. We flee from time. And from Cupid too. They have us in their power.

– And now? What is she doing now?

– Nothing. She stands. The notes are played. Or will be played. The music is completed. For a moment she hears it all.

– She remembers it?

– Her body remembers.

– And she will not talk to us? She will not tell us what she feels?

– No. We belong outside. We can talk to each other but not to her.

– Is there no hope for us then? No hope at all?

– Perhaps. Perhaps when we turn away the echo will remain. The echo of her face, the room, that cube of light. As for her the echo of the fields outside, of the music, of the painting on the wall behind her.

– All we have to do then is turn away?

– Who knows? There is no certainty. There is only the source. The source of light.

– Are we the source of light?

– No. We are only the eyes that see. The voices that talk.

– Are you saying that without us she cannot exist?

– No. I am not saying that. She can and does. Perhaps without her though it is we who cannot exist. Perhaps she has heard us. Perhaps she has become aware of our presence, here, outside. But only fleetingly. We have become part of the echo, part of the music, the music of light, echoing in the silent room.

– What shall we do then? What shall we do now?

– Who knows? Perhaps when we turn away the echo will remain.

– What must we do for that to happen?

– We must stop talking. We must listen. We must keep still.

– But if we do that won't we forget? Won't we start to think of other things?

– Yes, that too is possible. Even likely. But it is also possible that the echo will return. As echoes do.

Children's Voices

– What we should do is invent a game.

– What sort of game?

– I don't know. There must be lots of games.

– We've played all the games.

– That's what I mean. We need to invent a new one.

– What about that game with the letters and the blindfold?

– No. We must invent a game. A completely new game.

– Do you mean a game with a ball or with paper and things?

– It could be that. Or it could be different.

– How can we invent a game? We're not clever enough.

– You don't have to be clever. You just need to stop and think for a bit about what you would really like.

– Well you stop and think. We'll watch you.

– No, he's right. We just need to stop a bit and think about what we really want to play.

– I don't mind. I don't mind what I play.

– But some games are better than others, aren't they? Why should we just play other people's games. Simon's right. They may not be the ones we really want to play. Not really.

– How can we know what we want to play until we've tried it out?

– Oh shut up all of you. Either we concentrate and think of a new game or we give up and play one of the boring old ones.

– I don't want to play anything at all.

– Why not?

– I just don't.

– You can't just not want to. There must be a reason.

– Why should there be a reason?

– Hey! You know what?

– What?

– I think there's someone at the door, listening to us.

– Oh? Are you sure?

– Wait. Listen.

– I can't hear anything.

– Can't you? Listen.

– Do you know who it is?

– Of course we know.

– Is it him?

– Who else?

– He's standing there behind the door. Stooping down and putting his ear against the wood.

– Has he got his sandals on?

– Of course he has. He always wears his sandals. When it's cold he puts on socks, but he always wears his sandals.

– What else is he wearing?

– He's got his white pullover on that always looks dirty and his trousers hang down because he doesn't wear a belt. What else do you want to know?

– Do you think he realized we were talking for his benefit at the start?

– Are you saying that for his benefit now?

– No. For ours.

– Why ours?

– Work it out.

– Haven't we had enough of him? Couldn't we think of something else?

– You mean because there's no one outside the door?

– Of course there isn't anyone. Who would want to listen to us talking?

– Well, who would?

– No one. Isn't that so, Jojo?

– Well Jojo, we're waiting for you to reply.

– Jojo doesn't want to speak today.

– But Jojo must speak today. Mustn't he?

– Oh yes. Jojo must speak today. It is essential that Jojo speak today.

– Even if he doesn't want to?

– Even if he doesn't want to.

– Perhaps Jojo's listening to him out there in his sandals, snooping about behind the door. Perhaps he has ears only for him.

– Is that what you're doing Jojo? Are you straining your ears to catch a sound outside the door?

– Jojo doesn't want to have anything to do with us. Look at him putting his hands up to his ears.

– But we want to have something to do with Jojo, don't we? When he won't talk to us we stick little pins into his arms and legs, don't we?

– Even if he turns his back to us like that and puts his hands over his ears. We stick little pins into him all the same.

– Give me the pins. I know exactly where to stick them.

– You and Jeremy can do it this time.

– Why does he open his mouth like that and then not say anything?

– That's his way. That's his way of telling us he won't speak to us at all.

– That's all right Jojo. You just stay there like that. We'll sit behind you where you needn't see us. And every now and then Lynn and Jeremy will stick pins in your arms and legs.

– Not very often.

– Just once in a while.

– Just so that you know we're there.

– Hey! You know what I think?

– What?

– I think he's still outside, listening. Holding his breath and listening.

– In his sandals?

– In his sandals.

– Are you sure, Mary?

– He's standing there in his sandals and his dirty old white pullover, with his unshaven face and greasy hair, stooping and holding his breath and pressing his ear to the door. He thinks there's someone called Jojo in the room.

– Do you think he's really as silly as that?

– He's not silly. He just believes his ears.

– You know what I think?

– No. What do you think?

– I think he doesn't realize that he's in the room, and we're outside, behind the door, listening to him.

– Listening to him stirring on the bed, breathing, sighing.

– Listening to him straining his ears to catch what we're saying. Sitting up in bed, his eyes closed for greater concentration, turning his head slowly from side to side, trying not to make a noise, straining to hear.

– But all he hears is his own heart. The blood pounding in his temples.

– One moment he hears, the next not. One moment he could swear we were there. The next not.

– Now we'll all be silent. Now we'll all stop talking. We'll hold our breath and listen. We'll wait for him to act.

– Yes. When Simon gives the word, everybody stop talking.

– Now. Everybody. Silence.

A Changeable Report

TO NICK WOODESON

> Kent: 'Report is changeable.'
> – *King Lear*, IV. vii. 92

I HAVE been dead for five years. I say dead and I am trying to be as precise as possible. I do not know how else to put it. My hand trembles as I write but it is comforting to have pen and ink and paper on which to write things down. It is as if I had forgotten how to use a pen. I have to pause before each word. Sometimes I cannot remember how the letters are formed. But it is a comfort to bend over the white page and think about these things. If I could explain what happened I might find myself alive once more. That is the most terrible thing. The thing I really hate them for. They have taken away my life, though no court of law would convict them for it. When I think about that time and what they did to me, my insides get knotted up in anger and despair and I hate them not so much for what they did then as for what they are doing to me now, knotting me up with anguish and hatred at the memory.

I have tried to understand what happened. I thought that if I could put it all down on paper I would finally understand and I would be free of them for ever. But when I try I cannot continue. There is a darkness all round the edges. I think that by writing I will be able to shift that darkness a little, allow light to fall on the central events at least. But it does not work like that. It is as though the light follows each letter, each word perhaps, but no more, and in so doing moves away from the previous word, which is once again swallowed up in darkness. I pinch myself to make myself concentrate. I bite my lips and try to look as steadily as possible at what has occurred, at what is occurring. But the light moves along with the pen and I can never hold more than a small sequence in my mind at any one time. So I give up and wait for a better moment. But there is no better moment. There is just the urge to seize the pen again and write.

I did not think writing was so important. Till they shut me up. There was no cause. I had been gulled. But they bundled me in and locked the door. They told me I was mad. In the dark I felt about for windows, candles, but there were none. I was afraid of suffocating. I have always been afraid of that. I used to have nightmares about being shut into a basket and forgotten. I could hear them outside, chattering and laughing. I asked for pen and paper. I had to write and tell her what they had done to me. When they finally let me do so she had me released at once. I did not think I had changed then. I did not realize what it does to you to be shut up in the dark without hope or the ability to keep track of time. I vowed revenge on the whole lot of them. As I left I heard him start to sing. I went out into the night.

I had never had much time for his songs or his silly repartees. I do not know why she put up with him. Or with any of them. I need my sleep. I did my work well. I tried to keep them under control. I asked for nothing more. The noise they made. I could not stand that noise, that drunken bawling at all hours of the day and night. I cannot stand the sight of grown men who have deliberately befuddled themselves. It is degrading. Besides, she paid me to keep order in the house and I kept order as best I could. She should never have indulged him. Why put up even with a cousin if he consistently behaves like that? Why keep a Fool just because your father kept one? A hateful habit, demeaning to both parties. Let the Spaniards retain the custom, they are little better than beasts themselves. But that she should do so! And a foolish Fool at that. A knave. As bad as the rest of them, Maria and the cousin and his idiot friend. The noise they made. The songs they sang. Obscene. Meaningless. Vapid. Why did she let them? If it had been me I would soon have sent them packing. Restored some decency

to the house. And her still in mourning for her brother.
I thought she had more sense. A page. A mere boy. Get him
into bed at any cost. Forget her brother. Forget the injunctions
of her father. What kind of life do humans want to lead, what
kind of a –

My stomach has knotted up again. I hate them for making
me hate in this way. I hate them for doing this to me. When I
walked out into the night he was singing about the wind and
the rain. I thought I would be revenged on them all. My
stomach was knotted with anger. I wanted to scream, to kick
and punch them, him especially, the fat cousin, the –

I have said to myself that I will keep calm. I have promised
myself that I will control myself and write it all down so that I
may understand and be free of the darkness. I am a survivor. I
have not survived so long without learning a little about how
it is done. I have the will. I have the patience. They think only
of the moment. They drink and joke and sing. They did this to
me. They tried to make me mad. They tried to persuade me
that I was mad. They could not bear to have me there, watching
them, I –

At moments, as I write, I no longer know who I am. It feels
as though all this had happened to someone else and it had
simply been reported to me. I see things in my head. My
stomach knots in pain and anger. But I am not sure if my head
and stomach belong to the same person.

Never mind. I must use what skills I have and not be deflected.
I must be patient. Men have burrowed out of dungeons with
nothing but a nail-file. What are five years or ten years when
life itself is at stake? I have always been patient. I have my pen
and paper and I can always start again. And again and again
until the darkness is dispersed and I can emerge into the light
once more and live.

I remember the man I was. But he is like a puppet. I do not
know what kept him going. Perhaps it was nothing except a
sense of duty. I see him bustle. He was a great bustler. I
sometimes think I am still there. That I still work there, do
what I have to do about the house, take orders from him, from

the boy now, while she stands simpering by. I hate her for
that, for what she let them do to me and for standing by now
and doting on that boy.

But I am not there. I know I am not there. I turned my back
on them forever and walked out, vowing revenge. Yet I was
not interested in revenge. I only wanted to forget them. To
start again elsewhere. But I could not. The song would not let
me go. It was like a leash he had attached to me when he saw
that I was determined to go. I sleep and it comes to me in my
dreams. I wake and it creeps up on me in the daytime. I plotted
revenge. I thought I would find my way back there and take
up my post with them again. I would steal her handkerchief
and poison his mind. He would have killed her for that. Killed
her first and then himself. He was capable of it, he went for
Andrew the minute he saw him, broke his head and then
lamed Toby. They would have taken me back. I know how
she felt about me. I would have played on those feelings. I
would have made him kill her and then in despair, he would
have done away with himself.

At other moments I thought of other, sillier kinds of revenge.
I would have them all on an island. I would be able to control
the winds and the waves. I would wreck them on my island.
The drunken idiots would be pinched and bruised and bitten
by my spirits, and the others, the others would get their
deserts – the whole lot of them. I would frighten them with
ghosts made of old sheets, I would lead them into swamps and
then reveal myself to them – it would be the silliness of the
punishments that would be the most shaming.

Idle thoughts. I am surprised that I can remember them. At
moments they were there, so strong, so clearly formulated.
But I do not think I ever took them seriously. Because it was
as if I had lost the ability to act. As if his song had drained me
of my will. When it flooded through my head I cried. I cried a
lot. There was another music too, unearthly, and fragments
of speeches, but not speeches in the ordinary sense, not exchanges of information between two people, but somehow as
if their souls had found words. I understood what they said,

but not the meaning of individual words and phrases. In such a night was the refrain. The names of Cressida and of Dido, of Thisbe and of Medea came into it. The floor of heaven like a carpet thick inlaid with patines of bright gold. I remember that. It was like a music I had never heard before and never imagined could exist. And then I was in the dark but it was peaceful, quite different from that other dark, and there was another song, fear no more the heat of the sun, and home art gone and ta'en thy wages. It merged with the other voices, telling of Dido and Medea and Thisbe and Cressida. But when I tried to hear them more clearly, to focus on them better, they faded away and finally vanished altogether. I went out through a door and instead of the garden I had expected there was desert, dirt, an old newspaper blowing across a dirty street, decaying tenements. I turned back and there was the music again, but now the door was locked and I could not get in. Why do I know nothing about music? Why have I always feared it? Not just the drunken catches but the pure sweet music of viols, the pure sweet melancholy songs. I fear them all.

I tried to walk then but my feet kept going through the rotten planks. I put my hand up to my head and the hair came away in clumps. I knew this was not so. I knew it was only my imagination. I fought against it. They are trying to do this to me, I said to myself. They want you to think that you are mad. You will not give them that satisfaction. But I woke up dreaming that my head was made of stone and I held it in my lap, sightless eyes gazing past me into the sky. My daughter had betrayed me. She had stolen all my jewellery and absconded with a Negro. There was a storm and women spoke and tempted me. I looked at my hands and they were covered with blood. The storm grew worse and I was on a deserted heath and howling. An idiot and a blind old man held on to me, trying to pull me down, uttering gibberish, but I kicked them off, and then there was that song again, about the wind and the rain. In the rain my daughter came and talked. Something terrible had happened but all was forgiven. She talked to me. She answered when I spoke to her. But I knew it would not last and it didn't, she was dead in my arms, I held her and she weighed less than a cat. I pretended she was alive but I knew she was dead. I walked again and the rotten boards gave way, one leg stuck in the ground, it grew into the ground, and all the time I knew it was not so, that if I could turn, if I could return, and it required so small an effort, so very small an effort, then it would all change, she would be with me on the island and I would rule over the wind and the waves, she had only pretended to run away, only pretended to be dead. But I also knew that I could not make that effort, that I could not go back, that the door was shut forever, hey ho the wind and the rain. I marked the days, the years. I sat at my desk and wrote as well as I could on the white paper. I was determined that they would not make me mad.

It has been like death. Time has not moved at all. Yet it cannot be long before the real thing. I try to put it down as clearly as I can but there is darkness behind and in front. Nothing stays still. I cannot illuminate any of it. I form the letters as well as I am able, but I cannot read what I have written. It does not seem to be written in any language that I know. The more I look at it the more incomprehensible it seems to be. As though a spider had walked through the ink and then crawled across the page. As though it had crawled out of my head and on to the paper and there could never ever be any sense in the marks it had left.

Perhaps there are no marks. Perhaps I am still in the dark and calling out for pen and paper. Perhaps no time at all has passed since they shut me up. I call for pen and ink and paper but they only laugh and cry out that I am mad. I do not know who I am. Except that I am a survivor. I will go on trying to write something down. This is a pen in my hand. I hold it and write with it. This is me, writing. I will not listen to their words. I will not listen to that music. I will try to be as precise as possible. I will write it all down. Then the darkness will clear. It must clear. The music will fade. It must fade. I will be able to live again. That will be my revenge on them. That I have endured. That I have not let them make me mad.

Fuga

ONE day he took me round to see his mother and sister they worked as seamstresses I don't know the area exactly in the northern suburbs somewhere there are so many alleys and back streets but the flat itself was clean there was cloth all over the place and the wallpaper crying out it seemed like a continuation of the materials of the dresses the mother sat at a large table in the middle of the room he introduced us the sister had got up she was close to the wall I could feel she was frightened she brought us something to drink just for the two of us the mother didn't take anything and she didn't either something sweet rather syrupy but she wouldn't sit down nervously hugging the wall or fetching things he asked me afterwards how I liked her I sensed he wanted us to be friends maybe something more you could drop in when you're passing they'll always be glad to see you they're always at home he didn't say much to them didn't exchange many words the mother sat at the table in the middle and got on with the sewing the cutting I knew he lived at home but he didn't seem to spend much time there it was as if he was visiting them formally once a week that sort of thing the sister was cowering against the wall in her flowery dress against the flowery paper it was as if she was trying to disappear altogether she's shy she likes you he said afterwards she warmed to you did you notice how she sat and watched while you drank he wanted us to be friends and I liked her I felt drawn to her as I did to him though she was as silent as he was garrulous just drop in he said she is always there she will be pleased to give you a drink he even drew me a map with a cross for the bus-stop and another for the building that was how it started I found my way back I found my way there at first I liked it sitting there with the material all round and the two of them working away I tried to talk to her and she answered she always answered and so precisely but she never started a conversation herself I liked to sit there they seemed calmer when he wasn't there sipping the syrup I don't know what it was she would get up when I came and return with it and put it on the table and I would sit and sip and close my eyes and hear their scissors the mother never got up it was the sister who let me in let me out got up and fetched the syrup or answered the door but always pressed against the wall at first I found it pleasant just to sit there and talk so little and hear the sound of the scissors but after a while I wanted to see her in different surroundings a different atmosphere I asked her to come out but she wouldn't she wanted to but she wouldn't I looked at the mother but she went on sewing and snipping I asked her why not but she just shook her head for a stroll I said or a drink or perhaps they would both come out but the mother didn't answer and she shook her head and wouldn't look at me her hands rubbing rubbing behind her back twined together I asked him why she wouldn't come out he urged me to press her again confirmed that she really wanted to but didn't quite know how to accept and then all of a sudden it came to me that outside she would be nothing that she existed only against that wallpaper in that room with the mother sewing and the two of them busy that there would be nothing to say I tried once more but without much conviction I don't know why he comes now he comes every day why he brought him in the first place I had so much wanted him to bring someone to bring a friend anyone to see someone who wasn't him and wasn't her I liked the way he sat upright hesitant never taking anything for granted I wanted to talk to him but I had nothing to say he asked me out finally he asked me out I wanted to go but I had grown rigid she went on sewing I wanted to go I wanted him to take my hand and lead me but I couldn't go my body had turned to stone what would I do outside I know it here it is quiet it is peaceful I have something to do what use is walking up and down in the street or even holding hands there was so much of me that wanted to go but something held me my body was stone I knew then that I could never go though I wanted it so much I wanted even more to stay here to look after her to sew for him for her there was something that was stronger than every desire that held me that pressed me as if I had no other territory than this as if there would be no air in another place and so I shook my head and at first he pressed and I hoped he would take my hand take the decision away from me but then finally I saw that he too had accepted it and so it was mother sits there she has sheltered us she has fed us they sit there sewing the two of them I can see her turning into the wallpaper flattening herself more and more against the walls of the room until she disappears altogether I brought him round he was the only one the others wouldn't have had the patience I felt he was the only one when I first met him I told him about them I brought him round I left him there at first I had high hopes he came back regularly something seemed to be happening she was relaxing she was moving away from the wall mother sat in the centre smiling getting on with her work I think she too hoped we all hoped she came forward she even sat at the table with him watched him drink it seemed to be progressing smoothly inevitably and then all at once it was finished it was smashed as if in the end she could not do it though I willed her to and mother willed her to but this was her element this was the air in which she could breathe it was like a death for me it was like my death my own feeling that I too was locked here and perhaps it was for the best no one screamed it was all so quiet and yet it was the end of something the end of a hope but perhaps that is life the end of all hopes that is when real life begins the acceptance of life the life we have I stay out days at a time nights at a time and when I come home she gets up and brings the glass and the sweet liquid I don't ask anyone back any more there are just the three of us the scissors snap away I watch them sometimes I draw them as they work their heads bent or I paint the wallpaper the chimney one day I will paint her at the moment when she realized she belonged to the room the moment when the wallpaper claimed her it won't be about her it will be about me it won't even be about me it will be about mother silent and serious in the centre or about something else something only we can feel that is perhaps what I will do while they work to pay the rent to keep us here where we have always been where we will always be forever and ever just the wallpaper and the sound of the scissors and the silence.

Waiting

MARTHA, a widow, kissed her son first on the forehead and then on either cheek, both eyes, the nose, the chin, the ears and the mouth. She held him for a moment, then pushed him away from her. He turned, creaking a little in his new Army boots, and left the house without looking back.

After that, each morning, before she got out of bed, and each night, before she turned over on her side – the position in which she found it easiest to sleep – she said aloud to herself: forehead, cheeks, eyes, nose, chin, ears, mouth. Sometimes she added: shoulders, back, chest, stomach, arms, legs, hands, feet; shoulders, back, chest, stomach, arms, legs, hands, feet; shoulders, back, chest, stomach, arms, legs, hands, feet.

Letters arrived from the Front. She turned them over this way and that, then let them lie on the table. She repeated her litany, then tore open the envelope, pulled out the sheets, peered shortsightedly at the handwriting, hunting for the signature, then pushed them roughly back into the envelope. When she laid the table for the evening meal she would brush the envelope into a corner and then, when it floated to the floor, grab it violently so that the letter inside crumpled even further, and stuff it into a drawer as if it had caused her some offence.

She frequently sat at the table in the kitchen and counted aloud the contents of the drawers: knives, forks, spoons, bread-knife, carving-knife, ladle, saucepans, frying-pan, kettle. She lay in bed staring up at the ceiling and kissed her son again, holding him in her arms and then pushing him abruptly away: forehead, cheeks, eyes, nose, chin, ears, mouth; forehead, cheeks, eyes, nose, chin, ears, mouth. Then she turned over on her side and went to sleep.

In the street, walking to the shops, she went over the contents of the linen-cupboard in her mind: sheets, pillow-cases, blankets, towels; sheets, pillow-cases, blankets, towels.

Letters were infrequent. When they arrived it was many weeks after they had been written. She sat in her customary chair in the kitchen and looked at the envelope: forehead, cheeks, eyes, nose, chin, ears, mouth; forehead, cheeks, eyes, nose, chin, ears, mouth. Then she tore it open, scanned the writing, searching for the signature, and thrust it away from her: forehead, cheeks, eyes, nose, chin, ears, mouth; shoulders, back, chest, stomach, arms, legs, hands, feet.

She did not try to follow the course of the war from the newspapers or to listen to what people said in the streets. When it was over it would be over. Meanwhile, time had to be used up.

She laid out the crockery on the kitchen table but did not look at it as she went over it in her mind: cups, saucers, plates, bowls, glasses. And the cutlery: knives, forks, spoons, bread-knife, carving-knife, ladle.

She slept little, waking in the middle of the night and finding herself staring at a corner of the room with unseeing eyes. Then she would turn over on her back and go over it all again: forehead, cheeks, eyes, nose, chin, ears, mouth. After that, sometimes, she found it possible to sleep again.

One day the ladle was missing. She pulled out all the drawers, knelt and peered into the backs of all the cupboards. It will turn up, she thought. It's there, somewhere, I shouldn't have kept taking it out all the time to look at it, I should give up all this counting, memorizing, I shouldn't be so anxious.

But it didn't turn up. She tried not to think about it. She stopped herself reciting the contents of the kitchen drawers. Yet she went on opening cupboards, feeling in the recesses with her rough hands.

After that she had a dream. God spoke to her in her dream. His words were comforting but she had a sense of anguish, hearing him, mingled with a feeling of overwhelming relief. He towered over her bed, distinctly visible in all His aspects, a big man with a strong face and a beard, gesturing little but to good effect. His words poured over her like oil, continuous, indistinguishable, yet clear in all their implications. She stared up at Him in wonder, noting His white hair, powerful nose, regal body in its white robe – or perhaps it was light, a body made of light and not a robe at all. She was suddenly unsure, sat up to look more closely, and realized that one of His arms was missing.

The shock was physical: a blow to the heart. She struggled to understand what it was that confronted her and saw now that all one side of Him was dark, a vacuum. She wanted to protest, to say but You are God, no part of You can be missing, You must be all there, is this a joke or something? – only it was as if there was no longer any need for that, she knew now beyond all doubt, and, though His voice continued to roll over her in its soothing flow, she had ceased to listen, ceased, finally, to see.

That Which is Hidden is That Which is Shown; That Which is Shown is That Which is Hidden

TO ANDRZEJ JACKOWSKI

ONE day they found him under the bed, curled tight, pressed against the wall. For as long as they could remember he had been in the habit of hiding objects in boxes, in drawers, in holes he dug in the garden. Sometimes, when they sat down to a meal after calling for him in vain, he would suddenly appear from under the table. But when they found him that day under the bed it was different. He wouldn't come out and they had to pull the bed aside and haul him to his feet. His pockets were stuffed with objects: pebbles, a rusty spoon, two pen-nibs, a half-sucked sweet. When they asked him what he was up to he wouldn't reply. They pleaded, threatened, cajoled. When they finally gave up he went back to his place under the bed.

He was no trouble at school, did his homework, bothered nobody. But he began to spend more and more time in cupboards, sitting in the dark, or crouched in a corner of the pantry, behind the potatoes. In the attic they found an inlaid mother-of-pearl box with a cricket ball nestling inside. When they tackled him about it he only shook his head, so they desisted and hoped the fad would pass.

No one ever complained of him, but he was not interested in his work at school and left as soon as he could. He was never a burden to them, was never out of work, though he rarely held down any job for very long. One day he disappeared, and when he turned up again he told them he had found a room nearer his work.

In his new room he fitted out a workbench and began to make little boxes for himself out of bits of wood he found lying on dumps, and then more elaborate things, cupboards, boats, mysterious contraptions with shelves and holes and little passages and conduits, linking one part of the interior to another. Inside these spaces and holes stood little wooden men, sometimes with trays in their hands, staring straight ahead of them, birds with beady eyes, giraffes. The door into the dark spaces was always half open, so that the figure was both concealed and revealed. Look, he said to his mother. Look, look inside. And closed the little door.

The objects proliferated, grew more complex. He gave up his job and concentrated on his craft. He spent hours walking the streets, looking for likely pieces of wood. Sometimes he took trips to the seaside and collected hard grainy driftwood. Back in his room he sawed and chiselled and sandpapered. He used no nails, only wooden pins he made himself. The objects, looking like a cross between old butter-churns and complicated toys, stood in rows against the walls of his room. There is nothing inside them, he said to his father. And held the little doors closed. Nothing inside.

The room is empty now. He has gone, taking his possessions with him. In a derelict house, not far from the station, the police have found a number of strange objects: little cabinets with multiple divisions and, here and there, behind half-open doors, tiny wooden figures, round-eyed, staring straight ahead in the dark. The house is crumbling, deserted. The police take away the objects and then, when no one claims them, smash them up and throw them away.

There are no objects any more. There were never any objects. Now you know. Don't look for me. By the time you read this I will be far away. You will never find me.

In the Fertile Land

WE live in a fertile land. Here we have all we want. Beyond the borders, far away, lies the desert, where nothing grows.

Nothing grows there. Nor is there any sound except the wind.

Here, on the other hand, all is growth, abundance. The plants reach enormous heights, and even we ourselves grow and grow, so that there is absolutely no stopping us. And when we speak the words flow out in torrents, another aspect of the general fertility.

Here, the centre is everywhere and the circumference nowhere.

Conversely, it could be said – and it is an aspect of the general fertility here that everything that can be said has its converse side – conversely it could be said that the circumference is everywhere and the centre nowhere, that the limits are everywhere, that everywhere there is the presence of the desert.

Here, in the fertile land, everyone is so conscious of the desert, so intrigued and baffled by it, that a law has had to be passed forbidding anyone to mention the word.

Even so, it underlies every sentence and every thought, every dream and every gesture.

Some have even gone over into the desert, but as they have not come back it is impossible to say what they found there.

I myself have no desire to go into the desert. I am content with the happy fertility of this land. The desert beyond is not something I think about very much, and if I occasionally dream about it, that contravenes no law. I cannot imagine where the limits of the desert are to be found or what kind of life, if any, exists there. When I hear the wind I try to follow it in my mind across the empty spaces, to see in my mind's eye the ripples it makes in the enormous dunes as it picks up the grains of sand and deposits them in slightly altered patterns a little further along – though near and far have clearly a quite different meaning in the desert from the one they have here.

In the desert silence prevails. Here the talk is continuous. Many of us are happy even talking to ourselves. There is never any shortage of subjects about which to talk, nor any lack of words with which to talk. Sometimes, indeed, this abundance becomes a little onerous, the sound of all these voices raised in animated conversation or impassioned monologue grows slightly disturbing. There have even been moments when the very abundance of possible subjects and of available directions in which any subject may be developed has made me long for the silence of the desert, with only the monotonous whistling of the wind for sound. At those times my talk redoubles in both quantity and speed and I cover every subject except the one that obsesses me – for the penalty for any infringement of the law is severe. Even as I talk though, the thought strikes me that perhaps I am actually in the desert already, that I have crossed over and not returned, and that what the desert is really like is this, a place where everyone talks but where no one speaks of what concerns him most.

Such thoughts are typical of the fertility of our land.

He

HE heard on the telephone. His friend's mother rang him up one Saturday evening as he was preparing to take his bath and told him his friend was dead. The words went right into him, quite physically. He felt them entering his body, making no sense but leaving him with the certain knowledge that they would lodge there inside him like stones, that in the coming days they would insist more and more on his paying attention to them, and that he would never be able to assimilate them entirely. As always on such occasions the mind holds on to the little immediate practical things: Was she alone? Was she all right? Did she want to come straight down and talk? No, she had a friend with her. The police had just been and gone. They had told her that her son had been found dead in his room by his landlady. They would not say if it had been an accident or if he had deliberately taken his own life. She did not sound particularly anguished, she said herself that she had not yet really taken in the news, that that would take time, that she merely wanted him as her son's closest friend to know at once.

When he was eventually able to put down the receiver he found himself face to face with those first words: 'Alan is dead.' He knew he would not be able to digest them. He did not try. He phoned the dead man's other close friends and told them: 'This is going to come as a shock to you. I'm sorry. Alan is dead.' He phoned the woman who was at the time closest to his friend and told her. He was not prepared for her scream or her words: 'But I'm so full of him.' No one else that evening had spoken so directly.

He went to bed and, because he was at the time on antibiotics for some minor infection and the drug exhausted him, he went straight to sleep. He woke many times in the night and each time it seemed to him that he had not been asleep at all, but each time he promptly fell asleep again. He had many dreams, some of them so vivid that they seemed to be only the continuation of the events of that day. He dreamed that he arrived at the hospital where his friend had been taken and was shown the corpse. He bent over and listened to the heart: it was still beating. He called a nurse: 'He's alive. He's not dead at all.' The nurse called a doctor. Between them they revived the patient. 'You were going to have him taken away and buried and all the time he was alive and breathing,' he said to them accusingly. 'If I hadn't come along who knows what might have happened?' He was furious with the hospital, but there was a huge unspoken area of relief: it had all been a mistake; his friend was alive and well.

He woke from that dream convinced that his friend was alive and at once remembered that he was dead. He fell asleep again and was talking to another friend, a rabbi: 'You will say Kaddish for him, won't you?' he said, and the rabbi nodded. He woke, surprised at his knowledge of the word and once more aware of his ignorance of matters of ritual, Christian or Jewish. Did one say what he had said? Did it make sense? Do rabbis say Kaddish in the same way as a priest says a prayer? He was surprised to find that he, who had no faith and no instruction in any religion, should be so concerned with such matters at this moment. Perhaps it was that his friend had had a strong religious streak in him, though he could hardly have been called devout. Or perhaps it was that in moments like this we all reach out to the impersonal forms of prayer and lamentation, whatever our beliefs, feeling instinctively that they can carry the burden of our sorrow in a way mere thought or dialogue cannot. The next day he even wrote to another friend, a novitiate nun, asking her to pray for the soul of his friend and for that of his mother.

But it was not a time for writing letters. It seemed to have become a time for talking to the bewildered survivors. Every death leaves behind it unanswered questions, but a sudden death at the age of thirty leaves more than most. In addition, the facts themselves were confused and only emerged in fragments, as the police released another bit of information or the landlady remembered another detail and passed it on to the mother who relayed it to him. At first the weight of evidence seemed to be in favour of an accidental death. He had been going to spend the weekend with friends in Cromer, but on the Saturday afternoon the landlady heard the radio playing in his room. She knocked but there was no reply. She tried the door but it was locked. She called her husband, who broke down the door. They found him lying on his bed, covered in vomit, an empty whisky bottle and a full bottle of aspirin beside him. Though he was not in the habit of drinking alone it was possible that he had done so in a fit of depression and then gone to sleep and choked on his vomit. Moreover, if he had intended to kill himself it was likely that he would have left a note, and none had been found.

The next day, however, the information came through that there had in fact been a note, which the police had taken away. What the contents were they would not at the moment divulge. A post-mortem and inquest were being held and the truth would no doubt emerge in due time. The likelihood of suicide, however, was now strong. But if it was indeed suicide, why? Every one of his friends agreed that things had never been so good for him, that perhaps for the first time in his life there appeared to be a meaningful future ahead of him, that both his private and his professional life had taken a decided turn for the better in the previous few months. Could anyone think of a less likely time for him to commit suicide? His friends came and they talked and talked. For all of them suicide could only be seen as a rejection of themselves and of all they might have meant to the dead man. They could not understand it and they could not bear to be alone with their perplexity. The sudden death brought them together in a way the dead man, in the course of his life, had never been able to do. The talk was endless.

It was not till four days later that the police released a

photostat of the note. Yes, it was undoubtedly a suicide note but it answered none of the questions. It merely said that as he did what he did he thought with affection of his mother, his landlady and his friends, and that none of them had ever given him any cause for complaint. He listed his friends.

And yet, if this was the case, why had he done it? The post-mortem revealed that he had in fact taken enough aspirin to kill an elephant, washed down with whisky, on top of a meal carefully designed to keep the stuff down. There had clearly been nothing haphazard about the attempt. Always meticulous in his attention to detail, he had excelled himself here. First he had made sure no one would call on him unexpectedly by saying that he would be away for the weekend. Then he had phoned his mother and asked her to send a telegram to his friends in Cromer, saying that he was not going to be able to make it. A little later he had phoned his mother again to reassure her: he was fine, just didn't feel up to all that travel, he would probably go for a walk that afternoon, she was not to worry, he would see her at the concert on the Monday evening as planned. He had then had his meal, bought the whisky, told his landlady he was off, gone up to his room, double-locked the door, written the note, and swallowed the tablets. If it had not been for the radio he would certainly not have been found till the Monday night.

The talk continued. He found himself in the position of prop and comforter to the baffled and the hysterical – having them round, talking to them, calming them down, breaking the news to others, keeping everyone up to date with the details of the note, the post-mortem, the funeral arrangements. In a way this was a relief. He did not have to be by himself too much, did not have to face the alien thing inside his body: the voice over the phone saying: 'Alan is dead.' At moments he found himself wondering why people around him seemed so upset or why they put on such solemn faces to talk of what had happened. At other times, without warning, the sense of loss would sweep over him. The fact that it was suicide gave the event an additional dimension of horror: the thought of what his friend must have been through in those last hours. But it did not radically alter the basic fact that his friend was dead, that he would never see him or talk to him again.

Many feelings passed through him in the days before the funeral. Anger, at times: Why did he do this? Do it to me? And after we had talked so often about suicide and agreed that it represented everything we most firmly rejected? Perhaps, he thought, when he agreed with me, when we seemed most to understand each other, he was holding back, not revealing his reservations? Perhaps the belief that there had been any real understanding between them was an illusion? Certainly he now saw that he understood very little about his friend. True, there had been suicide attempts, but they had happened a long time before they met. In the previous few years, and especially in the previous few months, his friend had seemed to recognize that he had a great deal to give to others as a teacher, a writer, a person – and that in this giving a meaning could certainly be found for life. To deny this, to kill himself, was surely a sign that he rejected the validity of all they had talked about, rejected, in a sense, the very basis of their friendship. He felt it was a form of betrayal.

There was anger too at a more trivial level: How could you do this to your friends? How could you force them to clean up after you like this? You who had been so considerate to others all your life? And there was much to clean up: his room to empty, his clothes to sort out, his books to pack, his manuscripts and documents to file away. In that room the futility of it all swept over him: everything so carefully designed for living, for going forward, and then this abrupt end. It made no sense and despite himself he was furious with his friend for having imposed this upon him.

But such anger could not last long in the face of what had happened. He sensed, moreover, that it was only another manifestation of guilt. For after suicide everyone feels guilty. Everyone knows he could have done more – in general terms and also on specific occasions. It is these occasions which are recalled with the same painful insistance as one passes one's tongue again and again over an aching tooth. And the guilt is of course always deserved. We never do enough, always turn away, draw back, refuse to give. There are times, naturally, when we do give, and plentifully, but they never make up for the others, when we don't. If only, we say. If only I had done this, said that, listened more attentively, stretched out a hand. If only.

He had more than his share of guilt, for in those last months he had been so caught up in his own affairs that he had felt he was neglecting his friend. Yet friendship ought to be able to survive that. It should be based on the certain knowledge that even if at times the other withdraws, turns away, he is really always there. In times of need he is always there. And the fact was that in times of need the dead man had turned to none of his friends.

Such guilt is inevitable. But it is also an indulgence. It has more than a hint of masochism about it. He reasoned, as others did, that he had done much, more perhaps than might have been expected, for the dead man. It was an error to dwell upon what he had not done. He would suppress the guilt as he would suppress the anger. Neither was worthy of him or of his friend. And yet they both persisted. In time, he thought, they will go away. But the thoughts would not be suppressed: If only I had done this. Not done that. Been more aware. Less blind. If only. If only.

But even guilt faded a little in the face of sorrow. When he thought of his friend, of what his life must have been like for him to do what he had done, sorrow and pain overwhelmed him. He mourned for the loss of someone with such qualities of spirit and intellect, a good man, a good friend. For the loss of someone whose life, in the previous six years, had grown so closely intertwined with his. He would no longer come striding into the house for lunch on Sundays. No longer walk over the Downs on long rambles and short walks, with dogs or without. No longer be there to discuss ideas with, to show his work to, to thrust books at. He would no longer be there.

Yet even sorrow is not an emotion that should be cultivated. Like guilt, it is ultimately selfish: he mourned the loss of someone whose presence had afforded him pleasure, but in doing so was he not merely mourning the loss to himself of a part of the world? Such sorrow is easy to indulge in but it is very destructive. It leads nowhere. He wanted to suppress it, but it clung to him. He felt trapped, and helpless, unable to move forward or turn round and go back, drained of energy and drowning in guilt and self-pity.

When he became aware of this he decided that the only solution was to go away and think through the implications of his discovery. He understood that it was essential for his good to try and grasp what the death of his friend really meant, to him and in itself. He decided to go away as soon as the funeral was over.

At the funeral he was numb. There had been too much talk in the previous few days. He had ceased to feel. Others broke down around him or bore up bravely. For him it was merely a day to be got through. He did not believe in funerals or in churches or in the Christian notion of an after-life. He merely welcomed the event as bringing a time of speculation and uncertainty to some kind of end, as though his friend would only be truly dead once the funeral had taken place. Yet twice in the course of the service he felt a quickening of his interest, a flow of feeling running through him. The first time was at the sudden confrontation with long-familiar words: 'We brought nothing into the world, neither may we take anything out of this world. The Lord giveth and the Lord taketh away. Even as it pleases the Lord, so cometh it to pass: blessed be the name of the Lord.'

He did not know why this stirred him as it did; he only registered with some surprise that it did so. He was, however, far more violently shaken by a prayer spoken by the priest later in the service, and taken, he afterwards learnt, from a sermon of John Donne: 'They shall awake as Jacob did, and say as Jacob said, *Surely the Lord is in this place*, and *this is no other but the house of God, and the gate of heaven*. And into that gate they shall enter, and in that house they shall dwell, where there shall be no cloud nor sun, no darkness nor dazzling, but one equal light, no noise nor silence, but one equal music, no fears nor hopes, but one equal possession, no foes nor friends, but one equal communion and identity, no ends nor beginnings, but one equal eternity . . .'

Not since that first telephone call, when his friend's mother had broken the news to him, had he felt words dropping, as these did, straight through him to the centre of his body. And he sensed that they too, like those others would remain there, alien presences, demanding to be understood and stubbornly resisting understanding.

He went to the mountains, to a quiet hotel where he would be able to walk and think and write in peace, away from the telephone and the mail and the constant intrusion of those who meant well. It had grown in his mind that what he needed to do was write an elegy for his friend, a memorial that would be both a token of their friendship and the means of coming to terms with what had occurred.

He felt, obscurely, that what was needed was a ceremonious, ritualized piece, in which the personal would gradually be extinguished and reality – the reality of death, of his friend, of his own relation to death, to his friend and to the death of his friend – would gradually emerge. But as soon as he sat down to write he found himself involved in failure and betrayal. What he wanted was to try and make sense of a specific, a unique event, the single irremediable fact of his friend's death. But as soon as he began to write, that death turned into literature, another story, well or badly told, as the case might be, but still one story among thousands. Yet what he wanted, why he was writing, was to make himself understand that this was not just another story, that this was final, irrevocable, once and for all. And to *say* this was not enough. It merely turned the enterprise into a slightly more sophisticated story. He had wanted to use art to honour his friend and instead found himself using his friend's death as a prop for his art.

As so often in his struggle to emerge from the cotton wool of the self into the clearer order of art – for what was art if not a clearer order? – he tried to start with the immediate: with the cloud of anguish and confusion which lay so heavily upon him. But for once a solution failed to emerge. He was trapped in the cotton-wool. He could not put a sentence down without questions of style, of selection, of appropriateness, thrusting themselves upon him. He did not want to write more beautifully, more euphoniously, he wanted only to get at the reality of what had happened. But that reality remained hidden until he found the right words, and each time he rewrote a passage, scratched out a phrase, the futility of the whole business overcame him. More than futility, betrayal.

For example, to begin with something so fundamental he would not normally think about it at all, it would merely come with the first intense desire to write – in what guise should he himself appear? It would seem natural in the circumstances to use the first person; but that would in fact frustrate his efforts before he had even begun, since it would leave him lumbered with his own selfhood, his own confusions, his own inability to understand, when the object of the whole exercise was precisely to escape from that into a truer understanding of what had happened. Otherwise there would be no need to write, except as an act of piety – I came, I saw, I tell it now as it was – and piety he had no time for. On the other hand, to use the impersonal 'he' threatened to turn the entire event into a story before he had even begun. It is true that it might be possible to use the 'he' in such a way as to suggest that what was essentially not a story had inevitably to turn into one before it could be told, and the reader might perhaps be driven by the clanging objectivity of the 'he' into an awareness of the unsayable truth. But this was a poor and desperate solution to the problem, and for a while he toyed with the idea of using the second person: that hortatory 'you' would perhaps act like some kind of spiritual tin-opener, prising up the lid of his consciousness as he was writing, forcing him into a clearer apprehension of the truth. However, he soon came to the conclusion that this was far too self-conscious and literary a device. Much more than the other two it would draw the reader's attention to the work and to its author instead of making him focus more lucidly on the event he wished to illuminate.

Nor was this question of the personal pronoun the only one. Whether he decided to present himself as 'I' or 'he', there was still the problem of situating himself in relation to his friend. His friend had made an end, had found a place where time and space coincided for him at last. But what end can there be for a memory or a lament? And what part of space can the survivors be said to occupy? Where am I? he thought, in relation to the dead man and to the elegy I want to write? Am I on my knees in church, on a bench looking out at the sea, sitting at my desk or lying in bed? Whose mouth is it that says these words, whose hand writes them out? And with that the whole question of the pronouns was upon him again, and the cloud and the cotton-wool and the unappeased anguish.

It was in this mood that the words of Donne's sermon came back into his mind: 'And into that gate they shall enter, and in that house they shall dwell, where there shall be no darkness nor dazzling, but one equal light, no noise nor silence, but one equal music, no fears nor hopes, but one equal possession, no foes nor friends, but one equal communion and identity, no ends nor beginnings, but one equal eternity.' He spoke the words over to himself. Again, as when he had first heard them, spoken by the priest at the funeral, he seemed to be on the point of understanding something of great importance, but again, when he made an effort to grasp what that might be the feeling vanished, the words grew dead.

The cloud settled again. He knew that the only way to

dispel it was to write that elegy for his friend, but he knew too that as soon as he tried to think or write he was only allowing the cloud to settle more firmly upon him.

Death, he thought, creates a vacuum into which meanings and emotions rush. And when that death is suicide the process is accelerated a hundredfold. After a suicide everyone finds a dozen explanations of why it happened. No explanation is any more convincing than any other, we feel them all to be inadequate, yet we cannot bear to let the event pass into our memory without giving it some explanation. But because he had felt that every such explanation was only partial, the light it appeared to shed only an illusion, he had refused to play the game. In the same way, sensing the inadequacy and partiality of his feelings of anger, of guilt, of sorrow, he had tried to suppress them. But now he wondered if such a suppression of what was after all a natural reaction had not been an error. To deny oneself the freedom to find a meaning in an event because one knows one can never find the real meaning, to deny one's immediate feelings of guilt or sorrow expression because they are selfish and probably self-destructive — was that not perhaps to surround the central event with too much darkness, too much silence? The thousand partial meanings, the confused and sloppy emotions would lurk in that darkness, in that silence, unable to emerge but also unable to disappear. Perhaps what was needed was not to suppress explanations or emotions because they were false or selfish, but on the contrary, to track them down into the furthest reaches, the darkest corners of the self, and bring them to light. After that the second step, equally essential, could be taken. Once the meanings and the feelings had been recognized, noted and accepted, then it would be possible to eradicate them, extinguish them, burn them out in their entirety. For if too much silence is an error then so is too much noise; if too much darkness then so is too much light. Without the first step, the second was impossible; without the second the first would indeed be mere self-indulgence.

But how was this second step to be undertaken? He now

saw that it was precisely here that art came in. The process of extinction would in fact be one with the process of revelation. The work of art would bring to light what had previously lain in darkness and in so doing would reveal it for what it was: partial, confused, blind, egotistical. But by making what had hitherto been silent speak, it would make it burst and vanish. Once written out, neither explanations nor meanings would any longer remain behind to haunt.

The impulse of art, he now understood, is right: the impulse towards form, towards the articulation of pain and loss. But while recognizing this, we should also recognize the falsehood inherent in such articulation. To speak it, to write it, is always to get it wrong. But to understand our distance from understanding is itself a form of understanding. To grasp our inability to pay our true respects to the dead is perhaps a form of respect. Our art, it is true, clouds or dazzles, deafens with too much noise or too much silence, distorts reality with its beginnings and endings. Yet, if we will let it, it can also make manifest that which it cannot express.

We have witnessed an event. In this our life we will perhaps never be anything other than witnesses, even when the event is our own death. For what are we? We came into this world with nothing and we will leave it with nothing. Are we synonymous with our possessions? Clearly not. With our thoughts? No. With our language? No. We borrow words from the common stock in order to talk about ourselves and too often forget that the 'our' in that expression is only a manner of speaking. Of ourselves we are nothing, no 'I' or 'he' or even 'you'; only a potential that can be stirred into life by such impersonal activities as games or art, praise or lament. Through the gradual extinction of the mythical self to which we cling so blindly, of 'I' and 'you' and 'he', of anger and guilt and sorrow, we arrive not at a lifeless husk but at its radiant opposite, an animate potential which includes the dead as well as the living, where (for a moment) you are Alan as well as me, and I can be the three of us and you and I understand that this is both true and not true and that in this understanding, at long last, there is no darkness and no dazzling but one equal light, no noise and no silence but one equal music, no end and no beginning but one equal eternity. These things can be brought into being by art but they are other than art, that towards which art can point but which it can never speak.

He stopped in the silence of the hotel room and looked up from his page. Then he bent his head again and read over what he had written. For a moment, in the act of writing, he had thought he had succeeded at last in what he had set out to do. Now, reading it through, he realized that it was only another failure; and it was small comfort to him to understand as well that it was also the nearest he would ever come to success in this particular enterprise.

Volume IV, pp. 167-9

SHE was born in a small Austrian village a few miles from Salzburg. Her father was a baker and the smell of warm bread stayed with her to the end. It was not a good time to be born: 1928. She was the only child. Her mother died during the war, of fear and malnutrition. Her father went on baking. In 1946 she entered the University of Vienna. Obscurely, she already knew what her life would be like.

She took a degree in modern languages and then found a job in a big cement factory, dealing with the foreign correspondence. She saw the refugees pouring through Vienna but made no comment. Her stories had begun to appear in student papers, and then in the more adventurous literary magazines, in Berlin as well as Vienna. They were quiet stories, impersonal, level in tone. But their quietness masked an unease; or rather, affected the reader with unease by their very freedom from all sense of it. At the time they were described as 'pure', as 'classically calm', but their very purity seemed somehow to throw doubt upon even the possibility of classicism. All in all a surprising literary venture in the hectic climate of those post-war years.

After only a few months she left her lodgings near the factory and went to live with a painter. They had known each other at University. He was older than she was and had been married. Shortly after this she gave up her job, but the greater freedom this allowed her did not seem to affect her writing one way or the other. Her stories continued to appear, at the rate of one, or at most two a year. Quietly, they made their mark.

Four years, almost to the day, after she had moved in with

the painter, she paid a visit to her father, the baker. She sat in the back of the shop, as she had done as a child, and watched him at work. Afterwards, they shared a meal. Then she went back to Vienna, packed her bags, and caught the train for Rome.

The painter did not try to follow her. He knew it would not be any use, felt even that somehow, somewhere, he had always known it would happen. From Rome she wrote to him, saying that the absence of German in the air soothed her. 'My words on the white paper always look so unreal,' she wrote. 'Now their unreality is justified.' He would have liked her to say 'at least' – 'is at least justified' – but that of course she would never do. 'Is justified' was all he could expect from her. Indeed, he would perhaps have been disappointed with anything else.

Her stories grew simpler, purer. As though she would force reality to manifest itself by isolating the very essence of that which it was not. She lived alone, in a small but comfortable flat in Trastevere. Her stories had been published in many countries now. In the German edition they stood, three slim volumes in elegant off-white covers, on the shelves of all the libraries and bookshops. No one asked if they provided a sufficient income for her to live on, and, if not, for it seemed unlikely, how she managed. Her life, like her writings, was as it was. There was no room for questions.

One day there was a fire in the flat. Flames shot out of the windows and on the other floors women screamed in terror. When the firemen eventually succeeded in putting out the blaze very little damage had been done to the building. But in her flat nothing remained but a heap of charred and sodden ruins. And she too was found, burned almost beyond recognition.

Her stories sit on the shelves, four chaste volumes in off-white covers (the fourth was published after her death). In their simplicity and purity they give nothing away. Did she feel the impossible strain of that purity, that calmness? She always knew exactly what she was doing, no one had any doubt of that. She would know when there was nothing more to be said. Some of her friends maintained that violent action went against the whole tenor of her life and beliefs. They pointed to the fact that accident often played a role in her stories, yet accident so calmly rendered as barely to disturb the smooth sequence of seemingly inevitable events which her stories seemed less to create than to coax into visibility before our always myopic gaze. There is no such thing as a dead end, they liked to quote her as saying. When all the roads are blocked there is always another way round. It is merely a question of patience. Patience and attention.

For days, though, the smell of burning hung over the building.

Getting Better

THE first time Ivan caught himself dropping off to sleep in the middle of the day he shot straight to his feet. 'I wasn't asleep!' he said loudly. He had been dreaming that he was a stranger to Russia and someone – he couldn't tell who – was telling him stories about the country.

It's so flat, this person said. It goes on for ever. The roads are bad, they join one dirty village to another, one great big co-operative farm to another. In the central squares of the towns a clock strikes out the hours.

I know I know, Ivan wanted to say to this person. Who are you informing about all that? But nothing came out and with the effort to speak he woke up. 'I wasn't asleep!' he said loudly, shooting to his feet. 'Honest, I wasn't asleep.'

He tried to ignore what had happened, but it worried him. He wasn't the kind of person who fell asleep on the job. Luckily the colleague who shared the room with him on the top floor of the college library where the Russian books were catalogued was absent at the time, so he sat down again and rubbed his eyes and carried on with his work.

But he didn't like what had happened, somehow dreaded it happening again. And when it did, at exactly the same time, two-thirty sharp, the following afternoon, he went straight round to see the college doctor.

The doctor was a chess-player too, so they were acquainted. 'I wouldn't worry,' the doctor said. 'Between lunch and tea is when the organism is at its lowest ebb.'

'But I've never slept in the middle of the day,' Ivan said.

'I wouldn't worry,' the doctor said. 'The change of temperature may account for it.'

'You think so?' Somehow the news didn't exactly please him. He didn't like to admit that it was the dream or half-dream that had shaken him, not the fact of going to sleep.

'Who knows what stresses you've been under,' the doctor said. 'Falling asleep is the body's way of coping. Better that than forcing yourself to keep at it and then having something really go wrong with you.'

Ivan was unconvinced, determined to watch himself at those dangerous times. He couldn't even remember now if he had had the same dream the second time or not, but he preferred not to chance it. At night he was fine, slept like a baby the moment his head hit the pillow and woke up fresh the next morning from a dreamless sleep. So there was no need for him to doze in the middle of the afternoon.

For a few weeks after that things went well. He had two cups of coffee with his sandwich at lunch and then made sure he did a good deal of running up and down the stairs and bending at the stacks in the dangerous time. But one day, some weeks later, just when he was beginning to relax and think it had all been a question of nerves and he would have to watch that he didn't get into that sort of state again, he suddenly found himself leaping to his feet and saying out loud: 'No! I wasn't asleep!'

'Yes you were,' said his colleague, a dehydrated youth of Norwegian extraction who was working in the library for the summer months only. 'I moved your cup of tea aside,' he added, pointing. And Ivan saw the cup, which one of the porters brought up at four every afternoon, and which he had no memory of having drunk, with the soggy biscuit still in the saucer. He went to the window and looked out at the park so as to turn his back on his colleague. He looked out at the beautiful parkland but his thoughts were with his dream. Once again he was in a room with this someone he couldn't really see or anyway identify and this person was telling him about Russia. 'Every few miles along the main roads,' he said, 'they have look-out posts. Police. And in Moscow police control-points every two hundred metres.' 'Who are you saying this to?' Ivan wanted to say. 'I lived in Moscow every day of my adult life.' But again there was something wrong with the air in the room, when he tried to speak he couldn't, and the other waited patiently for him to finish trying, before going on with his account. 'Of course basically the country hasn't changed. And how could it, it's one sixth of the whole world, you don't change a sixth of the whole world in a day or a century.'

Ivan liked this dream even less than the first. 'It's not just a matter of falling asleep in the middle of the day,' he told the doctor. 'It's the dreams I keep dreaming.'

'You have bad dreams?' the doctor asked.

'Not bad dreams,' Ivan said, trying to understand in his own mind what it was he was asking for.

'I'm not an analyst,' the doctor said. 'I deal with what I can touch, John.'

'I'm not John, I'm Ivan.'

'With what I can touch, Ivan,' the doctor said.

But he must have noticed how upset the other was, because he added quickly 'If they're not bad dreams, what are they, to cause you such anxiety?'

'Someone is talking to me,' Ivan said. 'He is describing Russia to me. As if I didn't know.'

'It happens to everyone,' the doctor said.

'What do you mean everyone?'

'Describe what happens,' the doctor said.

'Someone is talking to me,' Ivan said. 'He is describing Russia to me. He tells me about the villages. The towns. He tells me about Moscow.'

'And so?' the doctor asked, puzzled, leaning his white head towards Ivan and twitching slightly in a way he had.

'I don't know,' Ivan said.

'Why does that upset you?'

'I don't know,' Ivan said. He waited for the doctor to say something, staring at the desk with its dark green blotter set exactly in the middle and the pen laid neatly just above it.

'It's as if he's trying to take away my past,' Ivan said.

The doctor sat back in his swivel chair and put his fingers together.

Ivan got up.

'You know,' the doctor said, accompanying him to the door, 'perhaps we shouldn't cling to the past so much. Perhaps it's a positive that you're beginning to let go.'

'It's all I have,' Ivan said.

The doctor held the door open for him. 'We must have another game, one of these days,' he said.

'I'd like that very much,' Ivan said, extra polite in order to take away from the nakedness of his previous remark.

So they began to play regularly on Wednesday evenings, when the doctor's wife was out playing bridge. Ivan was free most evenings and glad to get away from his flat in the town. Most of the time there was nothing for him to do so he stayed in and stared out of the window or read books he had picked up from the library that day.

He liked reading books about America. He asked the doctor: 'Have you been to the Grand Canyon?'

'Sure,' the doctor said.

'Is it wonderful?'

'It's a classic,' the doctor said.

Ivan wasn't sure what that meant but didn't dare ask. He was a better chess player than the doctor but his concentration was less good. In one rash move he would squander a brilliant opening. The doctor, hesitating a little to make sure his opponent really had blundered and was not enticing him into a trap, would shuffle his piece forward apologetically and then make a great fuss relighting his pipe.

'Holy mackerel!' Ivan would say. 'I've done it again!'

Between moves they would be silent, Ivan biting his nails, the doctor puffing at his pipe. But between games the doctor would get up and stretch and ask Ivan how he was doing.

'All right.'

'Any more of those dreams?'

'Once or twice,' Ivan admitted.

'Always in the middle of the day?'

'I never dream at night.'

The doctor let that pass.

'Perhaps you are right,' Ivan said. 'Perhaps I have to accept it.'

'There's nothing we can't learn from,' the doctor said.

'Even in the dream now,' Ivan said, 'I say to myself: All right. So what's wrong with his telling you about Russia?'

'Right,' the doctor said.

'Only it's wrong,' Ivan said. 'I feel it's wrong. As if he was saying I needed to be told.'

The doctor puffed at his pipe, cradling the bowl in his left hand. He smoked a sweet tobacco Ivan rather liked. Wednesday nights, when he took off his clothes to go to bed, the smell fluttered into the room like moths released from the fabric of the garments.

'I don't need to be told,' Ivan said. 'It's my country.'

'This is your country,' the doctor said.

'Yes,' Ivan said.

Now he was falling asleep practically every day, and some days more than once. He was no sooner asleep than he was awake again, leaping to his feet and shouting 'No!' He checked with Wallace, his colleague, who assured him the whole thing never took more than a minute or two.

'Your head suddenly nods,' Wallace said, 'and the moment it does so you start up.'

The doctor assured him it was possible to have even quite long dreams in just a few seconds. 'Most of our dreams are just recollections of the last seconds of sleep.'

Ivan took his word for it, had no desire to read Freud or any of the other people who had written about dreams. 'I wouldn't like to sleep on the job,' he said.

'You're irreplaceable,' Wallace said. He himself was leaving at the end of the summer, moving to New York.

'What will you do there?' Ivan asked him.

'I have plans,' Wallace said, and smiled his cadaverous smile.

Even in those few seconds Ivan went through a good many ups and downs. He tried to listen to the stranger with patience,

In the Fertile Land

with politeness, even with a kind of ironic condescension. But now the man had started showing him slides of the country. 'This is Odessa,' he said. 'This is the barracks in Kiev. This is taken in the Crimea, in Georgia, in Estonia. This is the Nevsky Bridge. This is a farmer in one of the Ukrainian co-operatives.'

'You don't have to tell me,' Ivan said. But though he could now speak the other paid no attention to him. 'This is Riga,' he said. 'The opera house. This is Novgorod. This is Tula. This is Vorensk.'

'They let you take these pictures?' Ivan asked him. 'You mean to say they really let you take all these pictures?'

But now the man was showing him a film. 'I don't want to see it, I don't want to see it,' Ivan said. It was a small projector, which made a whirring noise. The images flickered on the white wall of the room. 'I will explain now,' the man said.

'You don't have to explain,' Ivan said.

'For you to understand.'

'I was there,' Ivan said. 'I understand without your explanations.'

But when he woke up with that phrase still in his ears it sounded odd and false to him. He had a strange taste on his tongue.

He fell ill then and was delirious for a week. All the dreams came back to him jumbled with the images of the spines of the books he had been cataloguing. He saw his finger move round the letters and heard a sound like a mouse scratching behind a wall. The letters seemed to be in relief and his fingers walked in a forest of Cyrillic trees.

'You're getting better,' the doctor said. 'There's nothing to worry about.'

'I can't even remember how long I've been ill,' Ivan said.

'A week,' the doctor said. He didn't have his pipe. 'The temperature went down two days ago. I will insist they give you a month of sick leave.'

'What will I do with sick leave?' Ivan asked. The bedclothes pressed down on him and he lashed out with his feet.

'Don't panic like that John,' the doctor said. 'We must find you things to do.'

'All I have now is my work,' Ivan said.

'No no,' the doctor said. 'That's the way to fall ill again.'

The doctor leaned over the bed. The right side of his face twitched a little in the familiar way. Ivan watched as his mouth formed the words.

'You're an American citizen, John,' the doctor said. 'Your future is with this country. Don't take refuge in dreams.'

The illness was indeed a watershed in John's life. He still slept a lot during the day but his sleep was dreamless. In time he forgot his fantasy that he had lived in Russia and accepted the reality of the world around him. He did not even insist on the name of Ivan any more. Occasionally, it is true, as he stood with his back to the books, staring out of the big window at the campus park, he longed for dreams if nothing else. But he knew this was itself a sort of illness, a temptation to fall back into his unhappy muddled past, and he resisted it. Nevertheless it was perhaps the feeling that that past would always exist as a possibility which helped him to keep going in the country of his choice.

Steps

HE had been living in Paris for many years.

Longer, he used to say, than he cared to remember.

When my first wife died, he would explain, there no longer seemed to be any reason to stay in England. So he moved to Paris and earned his living by translating.

He was an old-fashioned person, still put on a suit and tie to sit down to work, and a raincoat and hat when he went out. Even in the height of the Parisian summer he never went anywhere without his hat. At my age, he would say, I'm too old to change. Besides, I'm a creature of habit, always was.

He lived in a two-roomed flat on the top floor of a peeling building in the rue Octave-Mirbeau behind the Panthéon. To reach it you went through the dark narrow rue St. Julien and climbed a steep flight of steps on the right, which brought you out into the rue Octave-Mirbeau opposite the building. There were other ways, of course, but this was the one he regularly used: it was how his flat joined on to the world outside.

From his desk, if he craned, he could just see the edge of the Panthéon. Every morning he was up at 6.00, had a look to see if the big monster was still there, made himself a light break-fast and was sitting down to work by 7.15. He kept at it till 11.15, when he put on hat and coat and descended. He had a cup of coffee in a bar at the corner, did what little shopping was needed, ate a sandwich with a glass of beer at another nearby bar, and was back at his desk by 1.30. At 4.00 he knocked off for the day and made himself a pot of tea – he kept a supply of specially imported Ceylon tea in a wooden box with a red dragon stamped upon it, and was very precise about the amount of time he let it stand once the boiling water had been poured into the pot. Afterwards, if the weather was fine, he would take a stroll through the city. Sometimes this took him down as far as the river, or even the Louvre, at others he made straight for the Luxembourg and sat on a bench looking up into the trees. He was always back by 7.00, for that was the time a table was kept for him in a nearby bistro. He ate whatever was put in front of him and paid by the month without questioning the bill. After supper he would return to the flat and read a little or listen to music. He had a good collection of early music and his one indulgence was occasionally adding to it – Harnoncourt he particularly admired.

Sometimes you went to concerts, his wife – his second wife – would interrupt him. He seemed to need these interruptions, was deft at incorporating them into his discourse. Not often, he would go on, too expensive and, really, after London, live music in Paris was always a disappointment.

We listen a lot here too, his wife would say. Friends who came to stay and neighbours who dropped in on them in their converted farmhouse in the Black Mountains, up above Abergavenny, were indeed often entertained to an evening of baroque music. His wife, a handsome woman still, with a mass of red hair piled up on her head, would hand the records to him reverently, dusting them as she did so with a special cloth, leaving the final gestures - the laying of the disc on the turntable, the setting of the mechanism in motion, the gentle lowering of the stilus – would leave all that to him. I'm so uneducated, she would say. When I met him I thought a saraband was something you wore round your head. You had other qualities, he would say.

In between records he would often talk about his Paris years. After his wife's death what he had needed most of all was solitude. Not that he wanted to meditate or brood: just that he didn't want to have to do with people. He took on more work than he could easily manage, needed to feel that when one piece was done there was always another waiting for him. Sometimes, in the early morning or evening, the light was excessively gentle, touching the tea-pot. I wouldn't ever have known moments like those if I hadn't been alone, he would say.

As he strolled through the city in the late afternoons he would occasionally have fantasies of drowning: a vivid sense of startled faces on the bank or the bridge above him, or perhaps on the deck of a passing boat at sea, and then the water would cover him completely and he would sink, shedding parts of himself as he descended into the silence and the dark, until in the end it was only a tiny core, a soul or knuckle perhaps, that lay, rocking gently with the current, on the sandy bottom. He knew such feelings were neurotic, dangerous perhaps, but he was not unduly worried, sensed that it was better to indulge them, let them have their head, than to try and cut them out altogether. After all, everyone has fantasies. In the one life there are many lives. Alternate lives. Alternative lives. That's the foolishness of biographies he would say, of novels. They never take account of the alternative lives we live alongside the main one. Like Shiva with his arms. In their converted farmhouse in the Black Mountains his wife would serve chilled white wine to anyone, friends or neighbours, who had dropped in to see them, always making sure that no glass was empty. You thought of alternative lives as you climbed the steps, she would say in her excellent English.

Steps are conducive to fantasy, he would say. Going up and down steps lets the mind float free. How often we run up and down the steps of our lives, like scales on a piano.

And always with his hat, his wife would say.

Yes. Always with my hat. On my head. I'm a creature of habit. I would have felt naked without it.

He had to explain to me that a baroque suite was not something you had at the end of a fancy meal, she would say.

And certainly she made life comfortable for him, saw to it that he had everything he needed, was not disturbed by any of the practical details of daily living. He for his part looked up to her, would do nothing without her consent, wanted her to say when he was tired and ready for bed, when he was hungry and ready for a meal.

He had been happy in his Paris flat. His desk was under the window and as he worked he felt the sun warm the top of his head and then his neck. If he gave his alternative lives their head he also knew how to keep them in check. Most of the time I lived just one life, or less, he would say. When he poured tea into his cup in the early morning silence it sometimes seemed as if all of existence was concentrated in that one moment, that one act. Could he have wished for greater happiness?

But do you always know what it is you want? What it is you really feel? Sometimes the tediousness and unreality of the novels he had to translate was too much for him. It was an effort to keep going till 11.15, and then he couldn't bring himself to face the afternoon session. One day, indulging his drowning fantasies more than usual, he did not go back to his room after lunch. Instead, he walked down the hill and across the river to the Island, and then across again and up in the direction of the Bastille. He must have walked for two or three hours, his mind a blank, because he suddenly realized that he felt utterly exhausted, could not walk another step. There was a café across the road, so he crossed and went in. It was empty at that time of day, except for the patron in his shirt-sleeves, polishing the counter. He eased himself on to a stool and ordered a coffee. When it came he swallowed it in one go and ordered another. This time he toyed with it a little longer, dipping a lump of sugar into it and watching the dark liquid eat into the white, letting it drop into the cup and stirring slowly, gazing down at the spoon as he did so.

By the time he had drunk this second cup he felt restored, wondered how he could have reached the stage of exhaustion he had just been in.

I want to make a phone call, he said to the patron.

The man stood in front of him, separated by the counter of the bar. He was a large man with a red face, bald but with a bristling moustache and large amounts of hair on his arms.

Could I have a token please. For a phone call.

He thought the man had not heard, then saw that he was in

fact holding out his hand, palm upward, and there lay the token on the creased red skin.

He looked up into the man's face again. The man was grinning, holding his hand out across the polished counter. He lowered his eyes again and looked at the token. There it was, waiting to be picked up. Gingerly he stretched out his own hand and reached for it, but just as he was about to pick it up he realized that it was no longer there. The large hand was open, palm upwards, but it was empty.

He looked up quickly. The man was still grinning. He lowered his eyes again, and as he did so the man slowly turned his hand over, and there was the token again, a small silver circle, lying on the back of the hand. The man thrust his arm forward again, as if to say, Go on, take it. So, once again he watched his own hand going out to meet the other, and this time the fingers closed round the token and he lifted it off the hand and drew it back towards him. As he did so he saw the hole. It was a small round black hole in the middle of the man's hand, just where the token had been. It was smoking gently.

He must have walked a lot more after that. He didn't remember where or for how long, but towards the end of the afternoon he found himself by the river again. He tried to look at the books on sale on the quays, but his mind wouldn't focus. He didn't want to go back to the flat, but his feet were hurting badly and he felt he had to take his shoes off or he would start to cry. He found some steps and staggered down them to the level of the water. There was a patch of grass at the bottom where a tree grew under the high wall. He sat down slowly, leaning back against the tree, closed his eyes, and fumbled with the laces of his shoes. When his feet were at last free he opened his eyes again and sat motionless, staring down into the water.

When the girl came it had grown almost dark. He couldn't make out her face clearly, only the mass of red hair that fell down to her shoulders under a little green beret. For a moment, in the half-light, she reminded him of his dead wife.

He must have spoken because she said at once:

You are English.

How did you guess?

I guess.

He couldn't place her accent.

It's hot today, she said in English.

Are *you* English?

She shrugged.

I too will take off my shoes, she said.

He wanted to talk about the token but checked himself.

She took off her beret: Hold it please.

She brushed her hair hard, moving her head in time to the strokes. Then the brush vanished as abruptly as it had appeared, and she took the beret back from him and carefully put it on, though this time at rather more of an angle than it had previously been.

He was looking at the lights of the city reflected in the river when she said to him: Do you mind if I put my head on your lap? Without waiting for a reply she did so, quickly settling into position and tucking her legs under her skirt.

Her eyes were closed and he thought she had gone to sleep, but then she began to move her head on his lap, slowly at first, as though trying to find the most comfortable position, then with gathering violence. He stroked her hair; the beret fell off; she began to moan.

They must have got up together. He could remember nothing except that her room was red. Like fire, she said.

He found himself walking again, swaying like a drunkard. His trousers felt too tight, his thighs itched where they rubbed. His body seemed to have been scraped raw from neck to crotch. When he finally stumbled home he was so tired he could hardly get the key into the lock. He fell on the bed fully clothed and was asleep at once.

When he woke it was dark. He didn't know if he had slept for eight hours or thirty-two. To judge from his hunger it was probably the latter. He found some food in the fridge and wolfed it down. Then he got into his pyjamas and crawled into bed again.

The next time he woke it was early morning. He groped his way out of bed and to the window of the study for his daily look at the Panthéon. It was as he was doing so, craning a little to the left as usual, that he suddenly remembered that all had not been entirely normal in the past few days. Alternative lives, he thought to himself, made his breakfast and settled down to the novel on his desk.

It was only that evening, as he was having a bath, that he saw the wound in his thigh. It was a long straight cut, like a cat's scratch, and it ran all the way from the top of his thigh to his knee. He touched it but it didn't hurt. He dried it carefully, examined it again, and decided that there was nothing to do but let it heal and disappear. In fact though it never healed. Years later, in Wales, whenever he talked of his Paris days he would point to his leg and laugh and say: It never healed.

You didn't want it to, his wife would say. Friends who had known him in the old days would comment on the resemblance between his two wives. Especially when she stood in the middle of the room like that, dusting a record before handing it to him, saying: You didn't want it to, really. No, he would say, looking up at her. No I didn't did I?

He's so superstitious, she would say. He never went to a doctor about it.

What could a doctor do?

Maybe give you something to get rid of it.

We've all got something like that somewhere on our bodies, he would say. Maybe if we got rid of it we wouldn't be ourselves any more, who knows?

Who knows? his wife would echo.

He would tell of his fantasies of drowning, vivid images he experienced at that time, when he was living in Paris after the death of his first wife. As I sank I would feel quite relieved. I would think: There goes another life – and know I had not finished with this one.

One sprouts many lives, he would say, and look at her and smile. One is a murderer. One an incendiary. One a suicide.

One lives in London. One in Paris. One in New York.

One, One, One, she would echo, mocking him.

With his soft grey hat pulled low over his eyes, he climbs the steps out of the rue St-Julien.

Exile

WHEN the letter arrived from my sister informing me that she was coming I cannot say that I was altogether happy. Of course I have always been glad to see her. Once we were very close, but when you live as far apart as we have for the past few years it is difficult to keep such a relationship going. I must confess that I could not even, at first, remember just what she looked like, and wondered whether I would recognize her at the station. I was surprised too that they had let her come, since in the early days she had moved heaven and earth to be allowed to do so, but without success. Yet now she wrote that she was on her way, and with vital news which she could only impart in person.

Suddenly the little town no longer seemed familiar. I had grown so used to it that I had entirely ceased to notice it, but in the days that followed the arrival of her letter I began to see it as she would see it, and I knew she would have little good to say for it. I tried hard to remember how it had struck me when I had first arrived, but you cannot simply wish away so many thousand days, pretend they have not happened. And the truth is that I had come to terms with the town. With the fact that it had nothing distinctive about it, not a hill or a river or a park even, that it was freezing in winter and, for a few terrible weeks in summer, unbearably hot. With the fact that the inhabitants were taciturn if not actively hostile, as though they had seen too many of us in the past few years and preferred to act as though we were not there. I had also got used to the fact of having nothing to do all day, though at first that was what I had dreaded most of all. I had in effect found a rhythm, a pattern. Every day I walked through the identical

streets with their rows of identical low houses and identical
wooden palings; stopped every now and then to watch children
clearing the snow from the tiny front yards; bought the few
provisions I needed; returned to the cold flat; cooked; sat
huddled against the cold for an hour or two, in the dark,
looking out at the moonlit town under its blanket of snow;
and tumbled into bed to sleep as best I could. For some reason
the satisfaction this programme afforded me was epitomized
by a peculiar sensation of peace and well-being which would
run through me sometimes as I lay in bed in the bitter-cold
pitch-black early mornings and stretched my legs out to opposite
sides of the bed, so that the blanket was pulled taut between
the toes of either foot. Curiously, in that moment I would
feel, in the intimate core of my body, that I actually existed in
this world of silent streets and identical houses, of white skies
and dirty snow, in a way I had not known myself to exist
before, in the excitement and hurly-burly of the big cities in
which I had always lived. And now here was my sister writing
that she was arriving, and with news she could hardly wait to
impart.

One train a week stops at our little station. It usually brings
people here; hardly ever takes anybody away. This is not a
place one leaves, either for a short time or for ever. You have
to learn to live with that, as you learn to live with everything.
And nothing once learned can be unlearned. That is the barrier
between those of us who have had to settle down here and the
rest of the world. It is not something you can convey to
someone who has not experienced it for himself. I tried to
explain this to my sister, as she sprawled on the bed in my
room and I sat on the floor leaning back against the door. But
she was not really listening. Her asking me how I was had not
meant to entail the kind of lengthy reply I was giving her. She
was anxious only to impart the news she had brought with
her. In the middle of my attempt to make her understand she
said suddenly:

– Listen. You know what I've come to say. You're free.

– Free? I said.

– Yes, she said. Free. You can pack your things and come back with me.

– Don't be ridiculous, I said. Her words didn't make sense. I didn't know which way to take them. From the moment I received her letter I had sensed obscurely that her visit was a mistake.

– Yes, she said. Yes. They rang and told me.

I tried to focus on her face but the room was spinning. This often happens to me in winter, when the cold is a perpetual misery and there is not enough food to stop you always being hungry. Finally I said – They'd have let me know.

– I was to tell you. You can come back with me. Do you understand? You're free.

I looked hard at her till I had got her completely in focus. Her eyes were gleaming with excitement. She was hugging her knees as she used to do as a child. I have always found it slightly affected in a grown woman, especially one who, like her, is running to plumpness.

– It's true, she said. They even told me you would get your job back.

I laughed. My sister has always been so gullible.

– Don't laugh, she said. It's true. I checked.

– Checked?

– I rang the paper. They said yes, it was there, waiting for you. They even asked me to give them the exact date when you would be back.

– You're joking, I said.

– Would I come all this way to joke?

I had to admit she wouldn't.

– Go on, she said. Pack your bags. We're leaving this dump on the next train.

– They're pulling your leg, I said.

– I thought that too at first, she said. I must admit I thought they might be doing that. I wouldn't put it past them. That's why I rang the paper. But no. It's correct. They're just waiting for you there. They told me to tell you.

– They're in on it then, I said. In on the whole thing.

– In on it? she said.

– On the hoax.

For the first time since her arrival she seemed nonplussed. As if she had suddenly realized matters were not as simple as she had imagined.

– Listen, she said. It's true. All you have to do is step on that train with me and you'll see it's true. I've brought money for your ticket, she added, as though that might be the complication.

– It's not true, I repeated. I won't let them do this to me.

– Do what?

– Humiliate me, I said.

– What are you talking about? she said.

I was silent. How could I explain?

– Come on! she said. It's true. I did not look at her. After a while she said quietly: – What do I have to do to persuade you?

– Nothing, I said.

– Oh, she said, relieved. I'm glad.

– I'm not going, I said.

– Not going?

– They're not going to humiliate me, I said. I didn't know why I kept on using that word.

– What humiliation? she said. What are you talking about?

I was silent.

Finally she said: – You're crazy. I can't believe it. You're absolutely stark raving mad.

– You don't know these people, I said. You don't know the things they do.

– They're not doing anything, she said. They're letting you go.

I shook my head.

– All you have to do is get on that train with me, she said.

Suddenly she seemed to sense defeat. – You can't not come, she whispered.

– You don't know them, I said.

– But you're free, she said. You can walk round the town now, can't you? You can eat where you want. You can come home at whatever hour you like. So why not just try getting on that train and see? If I'm wrong you'll learn soon enough.

– You don't know them, I said to her again. You don't know them like I do.

– You? she said, suddenly angry. What do you know about anything, stuck in this hole for years and years? You're the one who knows nothing. Absolutely nothing. And the fact of the matter is that you don't want to go at all, do you? You're afraid of leaving, afraid of facing the real world again, and you're even afraid to admit that, so you dress it up as cynicism and hard-won wisdom and pretend to be so much more aware of things than other people. Well, as far as I'm concerned you can stay here till the day you die.

How can you wave goodbye to your sister, even a sister you love very dearly, as the train puffs out of the station, when such words have been exchanged? – Remember, she had said at the end. Any time, if you change your mind. Write and I'll send you the money. But don't expect any loving letters from me after this.

The funny thing is I did expect a letter or two from her, in spite of what she'd said. I am still expecting them. But one learns to expect in a different way here. One learns to live with such expectations and one would be nonplussed to see them realized. Sometimes, when I find myself near the station in my daily perambulations through the town I go in and sit on one of the benches facing the tracks and think back over her visit. Though I had rather dreaded it in prospect, I must confess now that I was glad to see her. Her face as she sat in my room imparting her news, her eyes gleaming with pleasure and excitement, hugging her knees – that is not a memory I will easily forget. Indeed, it often slips into my mind at other moments of the day, as I take my walks through the little town, for instance, which I do every day, winter and summer. But never as I lie in bed on those bitter-cold early mornings and stretch the blanket out taut between my feet.

The Bitter End

TO JONATHAN HARVEY

Interviewer: 'Do you like
to compose?'
Stravinsky: 'Do you like to wake up
in the morning?'

HE is walking in a wood. It is early autumn but the leaves are already turning yellow and lying thickly on the ground. His mother comes towards him. He knows, though he couldn't say why, that she has come from the house, has come to meet him. She picks him up. He can feel her heart beating in her breast, under the ample folds of her dress. Her arms are warm round him. A tear falls on his face. It is hot and heavy, like oil.

He wakes up. Here he is high up above the city. The windows are closed. There is no sound. He draws a hand out from under the covers and touches his cheek.

The nurse comes in. 'We're awake now, are we?' she says. She goes to the window. Lets in light.

'How are we this morning?' she says.

She bustles about the room. Looms over the bed. 'We're looking well this morning,' she says.

The room. He has never minded what sort of room he had to work in. He has always prided himself on being able to work anywhere, under any conditions.

O. sits by the bed. She holds his hand in hers.

'It can't be done,' she says. 'They don't know what it means. That's why they have air-conditioning.'

'Take me somewhere else then. Where they open.'

'Windows just don't open in New York,' she says.

'Take me somewhere else.'

'Don't be silly,' she says. 'You know it's best for you here.'

'I feel I'm dead already,' he says. 'In this room up above the city with its sound-proof walls and its air-conditioning.' But perhaps he only thinks it, because she does not move, or reply, keeps his hand in hers and looks round for an ashtray as she is always doing. He has not known her without a cigarette in her hand and hunting for an ashtray.

The room is in darkness. His eyes have always been good but he cannot penetrate this darkness. He closes his eyes.

The pattern has not gone away.

O. holds his hand. The sun shines into the room. She holds his hand, sitting quite still beside the bed.

'He seemed better,' the nurse says. 'Yesterday he seemed better.'

O. will not talk about him to her. He feels her hand tensing round his.

'They're up and down an awful lot of course at that age,' the nurse says.

'We want to go away from here,' O. says. 'We want to go where you can open the windows.'

'You can't be better looked after than here,' the nurse says. 'New York has the best medical facilities in the world.'

'But the windows don't open,' O. says.

'The windows?'

'You know,' O. says. She makes a gesture with her free hand. 'Air. Wind.'

'The air-conditioning wouldn't work if you opened the windows,' the nurse says. 'Anyway, it's more hygienic like this.'

'How did people do in the old days?' O. asks.

'They died,' the nurse says.

'They die now,' O. says.

The pattern. Nine. He can feel the hum. One and nine and two and eight and three and seven and four and six and then five like a springboard at the centre. But that too is divided into nine. Nine small sections. And the fifth of these small sections subdivides again, it is turning very fast, whirling, he touches it with his hand, just touches and lets the edges brush the palm, tickling the palm.

The nurse pulls up the blinds. She turns: 'How are we this morning?'

He holds his hand out to her.

'What is it? What do you want to show me?'

It whirls. It strokes the palm, it tickles the base of the fingers. 'What?' she says. She holds up the hand. There are two sets of sensations then, quite distinct: her hand, holding his at the wrist; and the last vestiges of the whirling, the stroking, the tickling.

'What are you trying to show me?' she says.

She holds his hand up to the light. She lays it back on his chest.

'You look good this morning,' she says. 'I just hope I look half so good at eighty-five.'

O.

Her hand over his.

'Ah,' he says.

She takes the cigarette out of her mouth and puts it between his lips. He puffs quickly and she removes it. He squeezes her hand.

His father is standing at the end of the terrace. He is talking to another man. He gestures at him to come and join them. He starts to walk along the terrace towards them.

The two men have stopped talking. They are standing very close to each other, watching him approach.

He is walking along the terrace towards them. Beyond the terrace, on his right, is the lawn, and then the woods start. He can hear his shoes creaking as he walks. He can feel the cold stone of the terrace through the thin soles.

The word nasturtium.

A little train at the seaside, running along the beach. The word nasturtium.

The little hills. The valleys. Into the tunnel. Into the bend of the ess.

'Soon we'll have you back on your feet,' the nurse says. Her name is Elena. 'Call me Elena,' she says.

'I knew an Elena,' he says. 'I was in love with an Elena once.'

'You don't say?'

'She was like you too, in some ways.'

'You're teasing me.'

'My teasing days are over,' he says.

'Oh come on! We'll have you back on your feet in no time.'

'My feet,' he says. 'I doubt if they will ever want to have much to do with me again.'

The dark. Behind the word. In the little train. The sea on one side, the houses of the promenade on the other. A voice says: 'It is the back of nasturtium.'

And another pattern. Two quite separate stories. And then one is seen to be the back of the other. The back of nasturtium. The other reversed. So that they are no longer two. Yet not one. The train chugs. It is filled with children. Nasty. Tertius. Tertium. Tershum. A nasty cold. A nasal ort.

But why the train?

'What train?' O. asks.

'Train?'

She squeezes his hand.

'I smelled his breath,' the nurse says. 'You gave him a puff.'

'You begrudge him that?'

'You heard what the doctor said,' the nurse says. 'You want him to get well or you want to kill him?'

'I want him to be happy.'

The terrace. His father looks down at his shoes.

'I don't know why I was always frightened of Mother,' he says to O.

'I wasn't frightened of her,' O. says.

'I know.'

O. stubs out her cigarette in the ashtray on the little table beside her. She is smiling a little, to herself.

'It's him I should have been frightened of, not her.'

He puts his hand up to his cheek at the memory of the tear,

and then there is the pattern again. Nine. And eight and two *outside* one and nine. And seven and three *outside* eight and two. And six and four *outside* seven and three. And round the periphery, over the whole spherical surface, for it has become a sphere now, the five, the nine times nine times nine times nine elements of five.

The terrace. The house. The woods. Autumn leaves.

'Why do your shoes creak like that?' his father asks.

No.

Why these images? Why them and not others?

His father stands and talks to a visitor. He watches from the other end of the terrace.

Her arms round him. He buries his face in the warmth of her dress.

The house. The terrace. The curtain comes down. The audience claps.

O.

'The doctor asked me not to smoke in here any more.'

'You said he said you could.'

'Now he's asked me not to.'

'Ignore him.'

'No. I can't.'

It frightens him that she accepts the doctor's ruling. She has never stopped smoking for anyone. She senses his fear and holds his hand more tightly.

'We'll change doctors.'

'No,' she says.

He thinks: she could have gone on smoking so as not to frighten me. That she chooses to frighten me means that she feels there is hope. But there is no hope. She wants to give me hope even at the cost of frightening me. But there is no hope. She knows there is no hope and I know there is no hope. But then why has she stopped?

She has never felt the need to question his silences. To ask. There have never been any lies between them. Not where it matters.

How many little lies? How many unimportant lies?

So it is a play.

Now the curtain is up and the veranda and the house are visible again. Perhaps there are two curtains. Two plays. A play within a play. But the second play is identical to the first. The set is the same. The characters are the same. The dialogue, after a pause, continues in the same vein.

The characters step from the one stage into the second. And then go on with the same play. And when the audience is accustomed to it once more, the second set is also revealed as only a set.

What a bore.

His body has shrunk under the covers. He is so small he hardly raises a lump on the bed.

'We'll soon have you on your toes again,' the nurse says.

'I have never walked on my toes.'

'Oh?'

'Have you?'

'What?'

'Ever walked on your toes?'

'I can't say I have,' she says. She sits him up, helps him to eat. 'There's a good boy,' she says.

'Nurse,' he says, 'I am eighty-five years old. Your command of the English language must be somewhat defective if you imagine that a man of eighty-five should be called a boy.'

'Defective?' she says. 'Did you say defective?'

'Nurse,' he says, 'do I have to speak to you in words of one syllable?'

'Oh, I know what defective means.'

'You do?'

'Yeah. Sure. I was just surprised to hear you using the word.'

'Why should my using it surprise you?'

'I don't know. It just did.'

'Does my vocabulary generally surprise you?'

'There,' she says. 'You've eaten it all. We'll have you back on your feet in no time.'

'And what use would that be?'

'Use?' she repeats, surprised.

'All my life,' he says to her, 'I have dreamed about my work, and then when I have woken up I have gone to my desk and worked until I had got it done.'

'Oh yes?'

'That doesn't happen any more.'

'You don't dream?'

'Yes, I dream. I can't recompose it in words any more.'

'Why not?'

'I lack the will.'

'You could give it a try,' she says.

'Nurse,' he says. 'I have never *tried* in my life. I have either done something or I haven't. I don't know what it means to *try* to write.'

She is silent. Then she says: 'Why don't you write then?'

'I told you. I lack the will.'

'Perhaps for the moment you do,' she says. 'You'll see. It'll come back.'

'I cannot remember a time when I lacked it,' he says. 'In all my eighty-five years I cannot remember such a time. It is finished.'

'Don't say that,' she says. 'You'll write plenty of beautiful things yet.'

'Plenty,' he says. 'Of beautiful things. Yet.'

Why did the shoes creak? Were they new? Did they always creak? Or is it only in the memory?

'We were wondering,' his father says as he comes up to them, 'if you could tell us what the new rules are in the game of tennis?'

The doctor. 'I forbid you to smoke in this room. I categorically forbid it.'

Her fingers. 'Look at my fingers,' she says. 'I promised my mother I would never have nicotine-stained fingers.'

She holds her hand up to the light. 'I promised her that if I had to smoke I would always use a holder. She didn't want me to smoke but she knew we cannot always do what we should. She was aware of the virtues of compromise.'

A movement forward. Into itself. It starts. It moves inexorably forward. It arrives – at the start.

The dark. The silence.

He is walking forward. He is entering a room. He has been in this room before. When?

The dark. The silence.

The furniture in the room. The photos on the mantelpiece. He has been in this room before.

The photos. A man in uniform with a moustache. A woman with a dog.

The windows are closed. There is dust on the mantelpiece. He runs his finger along the mantelpiece through the dust. It leaves no trace.

The window. He looks through the window at the garden beyond.

He comes back to the photos. He picks up the photo of the woman with the dog. Turns it over. There is writing on the other side.

He cannot read the writing. He cannot decipher the words. He cannot make sense of the letters.

O.

She puts her hand on his, through the covers.

The room. The dust on the little round table by the window. He stretches out his hand.

Forward. One step leading to another. Till at last you are back at the beginning. But not a circle. A straight line. Straight forward into the beginning.

He says to O.: 'I was so frightened of Mother all my life. And now she comes to me in my dreams as the incarnation of love.'

O. says 'Not all your life. You have forgotten. It was only because of me that you were frightened of her.'

'She loved you.'

'You were frightened of her because of me.'

'My father was the one I loved. And now I am ashamed because my shoes creak as I walk towards him.'

O. Presses his hand through the covers.

'What nonsense it all is,' he says.

'Why nonsense?'

'I want,' he says. 'Oh I want.'

'What?' she says. But she knows. She presses his hand.

The nurse indicates that it is time for her to go. They stand by the window and talk.

'Open the window,' he says to O. 'Tell her to open the window.'

They do not respond.

'Tell her to open the window.'

O. comes back to the bed. 'If you want,' she says, 'we can leave here tomorrow. We can find a place where the windows will open.'

'It doesn't matter.'

'If you want.'

'It doesn't matter.'

Read it one way, it's one story. Read it another, it's another. First it's about him. A man dying. Then it's about me. I cannot speak. Not openly. If I speak it will be something else. Not this. It will no longer be about the failure of the will to live, about the final refusal to speak. So it has to be about him.

The dark. The silence.

It is always a question of finding the limits. Of liberating the possibilities of the subject. When that is found it becomes possible to do it.

The nurse.

'You know how I used to know a book was really there? Really going to get written?'

'I met someone who admires your work. A friend of my brother's. He was really excited to learn that I was looking after you.'

'I would have a sense of the book. The finished object. Of the physical presence of it. I would dream it was there on the table in front of me. I would open it and the title would be there. And under it my name.'

'He asked me if I'd ask you to sign a copy of one of your books for him, if I brought it to you.'

'And I'd turn the page, to see how it started, but I couldn't. However much I tried I couldn't. But I knew it was there. It was all there. All printed.'

'Would you do that do you think?'

'I had to get down to work then. That was how I knew I had to get down to work. I couldn't just turn the page. I had to make those pages come into being.'

'Would you?'

'Like tracing words that were very pale. Sometimes they were invisible. But I knew they were there. It was not that the page was blank. It was all there, but invisible. So I had to make them visible. It wasn't easy. But no matter what the obstacles I knew I would get there in the end. I had to, you see. The book was already there. It was already written. I just had to help it become visible.'

'If I brought you a copy would you?'

'Yes. Of course I would. For you.'

'I'll tell him. He'll be thrilled.'

'Now I can't work I don't want to dream any more.'

'He really will. I'll tell him. I'll tell him tomorrow.'

'Why should I go on dreaming if I can't get up and set to work any more? Why?'

'Perhaps,' she says, 'If we propped you up you could try one or two mornings, couldn't you?'

'I told you,' he says. 'It's not a question of trying. Do I have to repeat everything I say to you?'

'I'm sorry.'

'It doesn't matter.'

'Can't you will yourself to will?'

'No.'

'Don't say that,' she says.

'Why can't it all finish?' he says. 'Why can't it all be finished?'

'You're not to speak like that!' she says.

'What pains me, you see,' he says, 'Is still imagining. Still hearing in my head. Still seeing in my head. Still feeling the form trying to emerge. And then I can't do anything about it.'

'You're weak yet. Give yourself a chance.'

'Yes,' he says.

He lies on the bed. His body is so tiny it hardly raises the covers. He waits for her to finish and go away.

Silence. Darkness.

The patterns. They quiver, buzz. He knows that he must not stir or they will vanish. Though they only torment him now he cannot let them go. Yet, even so, though he is so still he is hardly breathing, they disappear. Trickle away.

O.

He has no need to say to her: You made everything possible.

She holds his hand. He does not feel it, only sees that his hand is lying on the cover and hers is over it.

She knows what he is thinking.

She knows that he is right not to hope any longer. She knows that he has always known with absolute sureness when something had to be started, when it was finished.

Of course there are moments of rebellion. Moments filled with impossible fancies. Moments when he cannot believe it is all coming to an end, here, in this room, with so little fuss.

But he has always known when to start a new work. When to stop. It has never been a matter of inspiration. Only of clarity of mind allied to will. Now the will has gone it is time to stop. To let it all go.

He does not want to go on. Not as he is. He does not want to speak to them any more. Not to any of them. Not even, he realizes with a kind of distant astonishment, to O. He has done with words.

For a moment he toys with the thought of that too as a pattern, and recalls the doubleness of that story, of the 'he' and the 'I' of that story, and then he lets it go.

I cannot speak the end of speech.

He watches with detachment as that pattern too slips away from him.

In his mind there is a very clear image: He stands on the quay, watching it go. Slowly, very slowly, he raises his hat and waves goodbye.

His body under the covers. He is so small now it is almost as though there was no one there.

He does not move.

He is asleep.

Distances

'Those feelable distances . . .'
                              – Rilke

A WOMAN.
    The sea.
    She begins to walk.
    She walks.
    She walks.

    The sea.
    She walks.
    She climbs the stairs.

    The sea.
    She walks.
    To her right, the town. Ahead of her, the gas-works.
    She walks.
    She walks.
    She climbs the stairs.

    The sea.
    She walks.
    To her right, the town. Ahead of her, the gas-works. In the
distance, the chimneys of the port.

She walks.
She walks.

She climbs the stairs.
She enters the room.
She says: – I've come back.
The man sits, facing the room, his back to the window, his face in shadow.
She says: – I've come back.
He does not move. He watches her.
She says again: – I've come back.
He makes a little gesture with his hands. Then he is still again, watching her.

The sea.
She walks.
A grey day.
The wind tugs at her scarf.
Ahead of her, the gas-works.

The stairs.
She climbs the stairs.

And again the room.
She stands by the door, her hands at her sides, pressing her coat in against her body.

She says: – I've come back.
In the bedroom: her suitcase open on the bed.

A cold day.
The wind sweeps in off the sea.
She walks.
The waves run in fast towards the shore.
She walks.
She walks.

The room.
The man has not moved. He sits, facing the door, his back to the window, his face in shadow, his hands on his lap.
She says: – I've come back.
He watches her.
She crosses the room and goes into the kitchen. She turns on the cold-water tap and lets it run, holding her hand under it. She takes a glass from the cupboard over the sink, waits, then fills the glass, drinks the contents down in one go, refills the glass, turns off the tap.
Holding the glass in her hand she re-enters the room.

The sea.
She stands, holding the railings, looking out over the shingle to the water.
Behind her, the town.
Flecks of sunlight on the waves.
She closes her eyes.

The stairs.

She starts to climb.

The man stands at the window, looking down into the communal gardens below.

She says: – You're not going to ask me?

– Ask you what?

– Everything.

He stands, holding back the curtains, looking down.

– You don't want to know? she says.

He turns from the window. He looks at her. She looks down at her hands.

On the bed, the open suitcase.

The sea.

She holds on to the railings.

The roughness of the surface where the paint has peeled.

She opens her eyes.

Flecks of sunlight on the water.

She turns. She leaves the sea. She walks into the interior of the town.

The room.

She stands in the middle of the room.

The man sits in the high-backed chair, facing into the room. His face is in shadow.

He says: – It doesn't matter.

He makes a little gesture with his hands: he brings the palms together, turns them upwards and away from each other, then lets them fall again on his lap.

The sea.

She walks.

On her right, the town. Ahead, the chimneys of the gas-
works.

She walks.

Her hands in the pockets of her coat, pressing it in against
her body.

She walks.

She walks.

And again the room.

The man has not moved. He sits in the high-backed chair in
front of the window, his hands on his lap.

She turns. She goes into the bedroom.

She stands beside the bed.

She moves her shoulders and lets the coat fall on to the bed.

She looks down at the coat, the bed.

A strong wind.

The waves chase each other towards the shore.

Close in, the white churning of the foam. Beyond, the
grey-black sea.

The room.

The man has not moved.

She says: – Please.

His face is in shadow,

She says again: – Please.

He says: – What?

She opens her mouth to speak. He waits, watching her.

– No, she says. Nothing.

– What? he says. Nothing what?

– Nothing, she says. Nothing at all.

The sea.

She walks.

Her shoulders are hunched, her hands thrust deep into the pockets of her coat.

She keeps her eyes fixed on the ground a few feet ahead of her.

She walks.

She walks.

She climbs the stairs.

She enters the flat.

The room.

Behind the empty chair the curtains blow gently in the breeze coming through the open window.

The sea.

She turns.

She walks away from the sea, into the town,

The crowds on the pavements.

She turns into a quiet street.

She pushes open a door and enters.

She queues at the counter. When her turn comes she says: – Coffee, please.

– Anything with it?

– No. Thank you.
She takes her cup to an empty seat by the window.
She sits.
She looks down at her cup.

And again the room.
She stands, leaning against the kitchen door, the glass of water in her hand.
She says: – You don't want to know?
– Why don't you take off your coat? he asks her.
– Yes, she says.
He waits, watching her.
– Don't you? she says.
He waits. His face is in shadow.

The sea.
Sunshine.
She walks.
She walks.

The room.
She says: – I tried, you know.
He waits, watching her.
She says: – Don't think I didn't try.
The curtains behind his chair blow a little in the breeze.
– I thought it would be easy, she says.
– Easy?
– I thought it would, she says.

He is silent.
— Just to go away, she says. To vanish. Disappear from your life.
— Yes? he says.
She waits.
— Go on, he says.
She shakes her head.
He waits.
— No, she says. Nothing. Nothing.

And again the sea.
Grey skies.
She walks.
Ahead, the gas-works. Beyond, in the distance, the chimneys of the port.

The stairs.
She climbs.
She reaches the landing.
She opens her bag, feels around for the keys, finds them, takes them out, holds them up to the light, selects the right one, inserts it in the lock, opens the door, returns the keys to her bag.
She enters the flat and closes the door behind her.

And now again the sea.
She walks.
Her shoulders are hunched, her hands deep in the pockets of her coat.
The wind blows the light rain into her face.

The room.
The empty chair.
She closes the door behind her and walks to the window.
She looks down into the communal gardens.
She turns back to the room.
She lets her gaze move slowly over the empty room.

And again the sea.
Sunshine.
She walks.
To her right, the town. Ahead, the gas-works.
She walks.
She walks.
Behind her, the stranger.

The room.
She says: – My legs hurt.
The man waits, watching her.
– My knees, she says. My ankles.
– You walk too much, he says.
She sinks down on to the sofa, facing him, and kicks off her
shoes.
– You walk too much, he says again.
– Yes, she says.
She looks down at her hands.

The health-food café.
She sits at the table by the window.

She bends towards the cup.
Steam hits her face. She closes her eyes.
The rim of the thick cup against her lips.

The kitchen.
She stands by the sink, a glass of water in her hand.
She puts the glass down on the draining-board and turns.
The room.
The man has not moved.
She sits down on the sofa, facing him.
She says: – I just thought it would be easier.
– Than what? he says.
– What?
– Easier than what?
– Than it proved to be.
He is silent. His face is in shadow.
– No, she says. It's not so easy.
He waits.
– What did you think? she asks him.
– Me?
She waits, watching him.
Finally she says: – When I didn't return.
He makes the little gesture with his hands.
– You thought I would, eventually? she asks him.
He starts to make the gesture again, then stops.
– Or that I wouldn't?
He is silent, watching her. His face is in shadow.

The sea.
Sunshine.
She grips the railings, her eyes closed.

She opens her eyes. Flecks of light upon the water.
She closes her eyes again, turns her face up to the sky.

And again, the sea.
She walks.
Ahead of her, the gas-works. To her right, the villas at the
end of the town.
She walks.
She walks.

Drizzle.
The health-food café.
She leans back on the padded bench and looks out at the
narrow street.
Drops of rain on the window-pane. People hurrying by
with their umbrellas up.
She bends over her cup and sips her coffee.
Her eyes are closed.
The rim of the thick cup against her lips. The sudden heat of
the liquid.
Someone is standing beside her.
She opens her eyes, looks up.
– Well well well, the big man says. Well well.
– Well what? she says.
– May I? he asks.
He puts his tray on the table and unloads from it a cup of
coffee, a plate with a slice of nut cake on it, another with two
scones and two pats of butter wrapped in silver paper, and a
little bowl of strawberry jam. He leans the tray against the leg
of the table and edges on to the cushioned bench beside her.
She moves closer to the window.

– Well well well, he says again.

He puts two spoonfuls of brown sugar into his cup and stirs. Then he starts to unwrap one of the little pats of butter.

She waits, watching his hands at work.

He removes the silver wrapper, presses it into a little ball, drops it in the ashtray. Then he cuts the pat of butter in two, slits open one of the scones and spreads the butter on the lower half. He dips the spoon into the jam, spreads jam on to the buttered half, replaces the spoon and lifts the half scone into his mouth.

He chews, stirs his coffee, drinks.

He wipes his mouth with the back of his hand, feeling with his tongue for crumbs at the corners of his lips.

– Why do you do things like that? he asks her.

– Like what?

He chews, swallows, licks his lips, sucks his teeth, wipes his mouth.

– Lisa, he says.

He puts his hand on hers. She pulls her hand away quickly.

– Lisa, he says again.

She fishes in her bag, finds a packet of cigarettes and a lighter, takes out a cigarette, lights it, returns the packet and lighter to her bag. She places the bag between them on the cushioned bench.

– If you knew the worry you caused us, he says.

– Us?

– You didn't think we'd worry?

She lets the smoke trickle out through her nostrils.

– Why, Lisa? he says, In aid of what?

She turns away from him and examines the drops of rain as they form and reform on the windowpane.

– Alma was frantic, he says.

– Alma?

– You know how anxious she gets, he says.

He butters his second scone methodically, lays on the jam, raises it to his mouth.

– What do you want? she says to him.

– Lisa, he says.

– You've got jam on your cheek, she says.

He rubs his cheek with his napkin.

– What were you trying to prove? he asks her.

– Prove?

– What did you think you were doing?

– Me?

– Me then?

He pushes the remainder of the second scone into his mouth and lifts the cup to his lips. He swallows down what remains of his coffee, wipes his mouth with the paper napkin and belches gently.

– Where did you go? he asks her.

– Here and there.

– You stayed with friends?

– Oh no, she says.

– We tried everyone, he says. Everyone we knew. We had to be discreet, of course.

– We? she says. We?

– You know what Robert's like. You know he needs support.

– Does he? she says.

– Lisa, he says, finding her hand again. Don't be like that.

She stands up quickly, pushing back the little table. – I must go, she says.

– Lisa, he says. Listen!

He puts a hand on her arm. – Lisa, he says. Please. Listen!

She squeezes between the table and the window and crosses over to where her coat is hanging up.

– Lisa, he calls out to her. Come back!

She steps out into the street. The drizzle envelops her.

He stares out after her, then pulls the table straight again, exchanges plates and starts to eat his way through the slice of nut cake.

And now she walks again.

The tide is out.

In the haze, far away, children play on the exposed rocks. Their cries drift back to her.

She walks.

She walks.

In the distance, through the haze, the gas-works.

She climbs the stairs.

In one of the downstairs flats a dog barks.

And again the sea.

She walks.

Flecks of light on the dancing water.

She walks, staring at the ground ahead of her, her hands in the pockets of her coat, her bag slung over her shoulder.

Behind her, the stranger.

She climbs the stairs.

The empty room.

She walks to the window.

She stands, looking down into the communal gardens below, and, beyond them, the sea.

A gull wheels slowly round, on a level with the window.

Drizzle.

She walks, shoulders hunched, the scarf on her head, her hands deep in the pockets of her coat.

Behind her, the stranger.

She walks.
She walks.

The room.
She crosses it and goes into the bedroom. She takes off her coat, opens the wardrobe, hangs up the coat, turns, looks round the room. She closes the door of the wardrobe and goes back into the main room.
The man has not moved.
She sits on the sofa, facing him.
She leans back and closes her eyes.
She says: – I don't know.
She opens her eyes. His face is in shadow.
She says again: – I don't know.
He says: – What?
– I suppose there just didn't seem to be much point in staying, she says.
He is silent, immobile.
Behind him, the sky has begun to darken.
– At least I couldn't think of any, she says.
– Any what?
– Point, she says.
– Ah, he says. I see.
– Do you? she says.

The sea.
Sunshine.
She walks.
She takes a path out of the town. It climbs above the cliffs to a little park. A few benches stand in the midst of small trees bent by the wind.
The park is deserted.
She sits down on a bench facing the sea.
She sits, not moving, looking out over the sea.

And again the room.

From out of the shadow of the chair the man says: – What?

– What do you mean?

– What do you want me to ask? he says.

– Nothing, she says. Nothing.

She turns again and presses her nose against the pane. The glass mists over and she steps back.

– Nothing? he says.

On the pane, a little cloud of mist and, in the middle, the mark left by her nose.

The little park above the cliffs.

She gets up from the bench.

She does not look at the sea now. She hurries down the path back towards the town.

Behind her, the stranger.

The room.

– You could take off your coat, the man says. Unless you're going out again.

– Yes, she says.

She stands, in the middle of the room, not moving.

He gets up. – Do you want a drink? he asks her.

– No, she says.

He goes into the kitchen.

When he returns she still has not moved.

He takes his glass to the window and looks out.

He says: – Don't you think you could take your coat off?

– Yes, she says.

He draws the curtain back with a finger and looks down into the gardens, sipping his drink.

The sea.

She walks.

A grey day. The wind blows off the sea.

She presses her hands into the pockets of her coat and holds it in against her body.

Behind her, the stranger.

She stops.

Behind her, the stranger stops.

She starts to walk again.

Again, he follows.

On her right, the town. Ahead of her, the gas-works. In the distance, the chimneys of the port.

She walks at an even pace, her eyes fixed on the ground a few feet ahead of her.

She passes the swimming-pool.

Behind her, the stranger.

She comes to a café, stops, hesitates, enters.

She stands inside the door, looking round. She sees a vacant table by the far wall and walks across to it.

She sits down and puts her bag on the table.

The stranger has stopped. He peers into the interior of the café.

A waitress is standing by the woman's table.

The woman says: – Coffee, please.

– Black or white?

– White, please.

The waitress bends over to scribble out a bill. Her yellow plastic apron crackles as she bends.

She leaves the bill on the table and goes away.

The stranger is standing outside the café. He rubs the pane with his finger but the steam on the inside prevents him from seeing. He straightens, then turns and starts to walk back in the direction of the town.

The woman sits without moving, the scarf still on her head. When the waitress brings the coffee she says: – Thank you, without looking at her or the cup.

The room.
It is empty.
The woman crosses it quickly and enters the bedroom.
She stands at the window, looking out.

The sea.
A light rain,
She stands, leaning against the railings, looking out over
the sea.
She turns and begins to walk.
Behind her, the stranger.
On her right, the town. On her left, the sea.
She stops.
Behind her, the stranger stops too.
She turns. She looks back.
She looks past the stranger, back towards the town.
She begins to walk again, in the direction of the town.
The stranger stands, not moving, looking out at the sea.
She walks past him, back towards the town.
He does not move. He stands, looking out at the sea.

She climbs the stairs.
She enters the room.
She says: – Did you see me?
The man has his back to her. He is looking out of the
window.
She says again: – Did you see me? On the front? As I
approached.
He turns to face her. He shakes his head. He says: – No.
He turns back to the window.
She says: – Please. We must talk.

He stands, his back to her.
She says again: – Please.
He turns.
– We must talk, she says.
– What are we doing? he asks her.
– What?
– I thought we were talking, he says.
– Please, she says.
He has turned back to the window.
– Please, she says. I beg you.
– Henderson's selling his flat, he says.
– Henderson?
– Do you know what he's asking?
– Please, she says.
– A hundred and ten thousand, he says.
– Why? she says.
– Why?
– Why are you . . .?
– He may even get it, he says.
– Get it? she says.
He is smiling at her.
– What? she says. Get what?
– The asking price, he says. He may even get the asking
price.

The sea.
She walks.
She enters the little café on the front.
She stands at the door, looking round.
The place is full.
She turns abruptly and goes out.
She resumes her walk in the direction of the gas-works.
Behind her, the stranger.

The stairs.

From the flat, the sound of laughter.

She opens the door.

– Well well well, the big man says. Look who's here.

– She came back, the man says.

– Of course she came back, the big man says. We had a cup of coffee at the health-food place the other day.

She waits, standing at the open door.

– Won't you close the door? the man asks her.

She says: – I'm tired.

She pushes the door shut behind her.

– Drink? the big man says. What about a drink?

He crosses the room. – While I'm about it, he says, I'll help myself to another if I may, Robert. Alma?

– Alma? the big man says again.

The dark woman holds out her glass.

The woman sits on the sofa.

– If you're tired, the man says, go and rest.

– Yes, she says.

The big man stands beside her, holding out a glass.

– She's got into the habit of walking a great deal, the man says.

– You want to watch it Lisa, the big man says. It can lead to all sorts of complications, walking.

She is looking down at the carpet. The big man is standing over her, holding out a glass.

– There's a table beside her, Bertie, the dark woman says.

– I'm not yet totally blind, the big man says.

– Well put it down then, the dark woman says.

The big man turns slowly and stares at her.

– Oh for godsake! the dark woman says.

– Whatsake?

The dark woman says: – Where did you go Lisa? Why are you being so secretive about it?

– She's not being secretive, the big man says. She just can't remember where she went.

He puts the glass down on a little table beside her and sits down on the sofa next to her.

She stands abruptly. – I'm tired, she says. I'm going to lie down.

– Come on, the big man says. Stay a bit and talk to us Lisa.

She closes the bedroom door behind her and stands, leaning against it, her eyes shut.

In the other room the conversation starts up again, softly. Then the dark woman laughs, very loudly.

Grey sky. Evening.
Black sea.
She says: – The empty sky. The empty sky.
She starts to walk.

Midday. Blue sky. Sunshine.

She walks up the path till she reaches the little park at the top of the cliff.

She walks among the deserted benches, the stunted trees.

She sits in the exact middle of the central bench, facing the sea.

Light bounces off the water. She shades her eyes as she looks.

She sits. She looks.

Morning. Grey sky.

She walks, her hands deep in the pockets of her coat, pressing it in against her body.

Behind her, the stranger.

She passes the swimming-pool, the miniature golf.

She reaches the little café. Stops.

She enters.

There is a vacant table by the window. She crosses over to it and sits down.

The stranger.

He stops outside the café. Enters.

He stands in the doorway, looking round.

The waitress, in her yellow plastic apron.

The woman says: – Coffee, please.

– Black or white?

– White.

The girl bends over the table, scribbling out the bill.

The woman says: – Don't drown it in milk.

The girl is turning away. She stops. She says: – You want it black?

– No, the woman says. White. I just don't want too much milk in it.

– There's black or white, the waitress says.

She stands by the table, in her yellow apron.

– Nothing in between? the woman asks.

– No, the girl says, looking out at the sea over the customer's head.

– I'll have it black then, the woman says.

– I thought you said white?

– I've changed my mind, the woman says.

– One black, the girl says, writing it out.

She crumples up the first bill and moves away.

The woman slips her coat off her shoulders on to the back of the chair. She takes off her scarf, folds it, lays it over the coat. She takes a brush out of her bag and bends over, brushing her hair. She straightens, puts the brush back and takes out a packet of cigarettes and a lighter.

The stranger turns at the door and goes out. He starts to walk back towards the town.

The waitress brings a cup of black coffee. She puts it on the table without looking at the woman.

The woman says: – Is it possible to have the music down a bit?

– Music? the girl says.

The woman waits.

– You don't like it? the girl asks.

– I'd rather it wasn't quite so loud.

– It's for atmosphere, the girl says.

– Yes, the woman says. Could it be a little less loud, do you think?

– People like it like that, the girl says.

– As loud as that?

– Yes, the girl says.

– I see, the woman says.

The girl moves away.

The woman takes a cigarette from the packet and lights it, looking out of the window at the sea over the flame.

The bedroom.

She stands at the door.

Very slowly she takes off her coat, walks to the wardrobe, opens it, takes out a hanger, puts the coat on it, pushes it into the wardrobe, closes the door.

She turns. She looks at the bed.

She crosses over to the bed and stops, looking down at it.

Through the open window, the sound of the gulls.

The sea.

She turns her back to it abruptly and starts to walk into the town.

She reaches the health-food café.

She enters.

She hangs her coat up.

She joins the queue.

She pays for her coffee and takes it over to a seat by the window.

She sits.

She lights a cigarette and closes her eyes.

There is someone standing beside her.

She opens her eyes, looks up.

– May I? the big man asks.

He puts his tray down on the table.

She moves to the edge of the little bench, pressing against the window. He edges in beside her with a sigh.

– I didn't know you were in the habit of coming here, she says.

– Didn't you?

He takes his plates, his cup, his little bowl of strawberry jam off the tray and arranges them on the table in front of him. He leans the empty tray against the leg of the table.

– I only came here because I didn't think anyone I knew frequented the place, she says.

– Ts ts ts, he says.

She stubs out her cigarette and lights another.

– You're smoking a lot these days, he says as he unwraps one of the pats of butter.

– It's me nerves, she says.

– You know it's forbidden in here, he says.

He takes a gulp of coffee and puts his hand on hers. – Lisa, he says. Listen to me.

She pulls her hand away.

He cuts open one of the two scones and butters the bottom half carefully.

– You're so aggressive, he says.

She laughs.

– Listen to me, he says again, turning towards her on the little cushioned bench.

– No, she says.

– You haven't heard what I was going to say.

– I don't want to, she says.

He spreads jam on the half scone and takes a bite out of it. He chews, looking at her.

– We two have got to have a little talk, he says, stirring his coffee.

– No we don't, she says.

– Lisa, he says, reaching for her hand. Darling.

– Oh leave me alone, she says.

– And we used to be such friends, he says.

– When? she says.

– Ts ts ts, he says again.

She drinks her coffee.

– Why did you vanish like that? he says. Without a word to anyone.

– I should have told you where I was going? she asks him.

– Not necessarily me.

– Ah, she says.

He attacks the second half of his first scone.

– How is Alma? she asks him.

– It's you I want to talk about, he says.

– You don't want to tell me how she is?

– Why shouldn't I want to tell you that?

– How is she then?

– Lisa, he says.

– How is she?

– All right, he says. Busy. As usual.

– And Carol?

– Lisa, he says.

– She's passed her exams?

– Of course she's passed her exams, he says. She passes all her exams with top grades. I want to talk about you.

– What are her plans?

– Lisa, he says. Do you know what you are doing?

– What are her plans?

– Lisa, he says.

She pats her lips with her napkin.

– Lisa, he says. You know how it is. I hate to see Robert

worried. I hate it. Then Alma sees me worried and she can't work.
    – What has that got to do with me?
    – Lisa, he says.
    She stands up.
    – Lisa, he says, putting a hand on her arm.
    – Let me go, she says.
    She pushes the table away and stands up.
    – Arrivederci, he says.
    – What are you talking about? she says.
    He watches her through the window as she walks away down the street. She does not look back.

    And again, the sea.
    She walks.
    Behind her, the stranger.
    She stops. She turns towards the sea.
    She leans against the railings and closes her eyes.
    The sun on her face.
    The sea.
    She begins to walk again.
    Behind her, the stranger.
    She stops. She turns. She looks past the stranger to the town beyond.
    The stranger goes on walking. He walks past her. She keeps her eyes fixed on the town.
    The stranger stops. He looks out at the sea.
    She starts to walk again.
    She passes him. He is staring out at the sea.
    She walks quickly, her hands thrust deep into the pockets of her coat, her bag slung over her shoulder, her eyes fixed on the ground a few feet ahead of her.
    Behind her, the stranger starts to walk again.

The sea.

She sits on a bench in the little park at the top of the cliffs.

The sea.

The cloudless sky.

She closes her eyes.

In the room the big man says: – By the light of the fireflies.

The dark-haired woman says: – Lisa isn't interested in fire-flies.

– How do you know I'm not? the woman says.

– I thought you were asleep, the dark-haired woman says.

– She's interested in a great many things, the big man says. Aren't you, Lisa?

– Not in fireflies, the dark-haired woman says.

– I'm interested in a lot of things, the woman says.

– That's what I said, the big man says. She's got a great many interests. But the law is not one of them.

– Why do you say that? the dark-haired woman says.

– Because it's the truth, the big man says.

– Since when have you been so interested in the truth? the dark woman says.

– It must have been some time in my twelfth year, the big man says.

– Thank you, the dark woman says. Now tell me why she isn't interested in the law?

– Because it's what I practise, the big man says. She's not interested in anything to do with me.

– Are you sure? the dark woman says.

– Positive, the big man says.

– I hear Carol passed all her exams, the woman says.

– She always does, the dark woman says. You can place a bet on her every time and you won't lose. I promise you.

The big man puts his scarf round his neck and picks up his coat. The man stands talking with him by the door till the dark woman joins them. Then they all three move on to the landing, talking.

The man returns, shutting the door behind him.

He walks back to his chair by the window and sits down.

The sea.

The woman climbs the little path up to the park above the cliffs.

She emerges among the benches and stunted trees.

Below her, the sea.

She walks down the alleys of the little park.

She stands close to the edge of the cliff.

The air trembles in the heat.

She holds up a hand, passes it through the air in front of her face.

She smiles.

The sea.

She walks.

People coming towards her swerve to avoid her. She keeps her eyes on the ground a few feet ahead of her and her hands deep in the pockets of her coat.

Behind her, the stranger.

She comes to the little café on the front, and enters.

She finds an empty table and sits down.

She takes off her scarf and shakes out her hair.

She brings a brush out of her bag and bends her head, brushing her hair with quick, violent strokes. She straightens and puts the brush back in her bag.

The waitress in her yellow plastic apron.

– Coffee, the woman says.

– Black or white?

– The black is acid, the woman says.

– White then? the girl says.

– The white is tasteless.

The girl waits, staring out of the window at the sea.

– All right, the woman says. White.

The girl scribbles out the bill and leaves it on the table.

The stranger is walking between the tables.

He stands in front of her.

– May I sit down please? he asks her.

– Do I know you? she asks him.

– I should like to talk to you.

– Why?

– I should like.

She takes the cigarettes and lighter out of her bag, pulls out a cigarette, lights it, returns the packet and lighter to her bag.

– May I sit down? he asks again, his hand on the back of the vacant chair.

The woman is looking out at the sea.

He pulls out the chair and sits down.

The waitress sets the woman's coffee down in front of her. She says to the man: – Yes?

– Tea, the man says.

He stops her as she is writing: – You have lemon tea?

– Only milk, the girl says.

– All right.

She puts the bill on the table next to the other and turns away.

– I should like to talk to you, he says.

– Why?

– I have been following you. I would like to talk to you.

– About what? the woman says.

– I would like to know why you walk as you do. You do not seem to me to walk like other people.

She stubs her cigarette out in the ashtray between them.

– Not the walk itself, the man says. But what the walk says. About you.

The waitress brings his tea. He takes one of the little packets of sugar from the bowl on the table, taps it, slits it open. He pours the sugar into his cup and crumples up the packet. He

drops the little ball into the ashtray.
   – Do you understand what I mean? he asks her.
She bends and sips her coffee.
   – I do not wish to offend you, he says.
   – I'm not easy to offend.
   – Good, he says.
   – Oh?
He stirs his tea. – There is perhaps something hunted in your walk, he says.
She laughs.
   – It's funny? he asks her.
She pushes away her cup and stands up. He does not move.
She carries her bill across to the cash desk and waits.
   – Forty pence, the girl at the till says.
The woman holds out a note.
   – You don't have anything smaller? the girl asks.
The woman holds the note out to her, waiting.
The girl raises her eyes to the ceiling, takes the note and laboriously counts out the change. The woman drops the money into her purse without counting it.
Outside she pauses, takes the scarf out of her bag and puts it on her head, staring at her reflection in the window of the café.
She turns and begins to walk back towards the town.

The stairs.
The room.
She leans against the door and waits, listening.
She crosses to the window.
She turns.
She looks slowly round the empty room.

And again the sea.
She advances across the shingle.

The beach is deserted. A mist rolls in from the sea, covering the town.

She walks over the stones till she reaches the edge of the water.

The tide is retreating, leaving little patches of wet sand behind it.

She stands close to the water, listening to the sound of the waves sucking at the stones.

The sea.
She walks.
A woman asks her: – How do I get to the North Pier please?
She turns, pointing.
– There?
She points.
– That way?
– Yes.
The tide is coming in. Gulls wheel and scream. The sky is uniformly grey, the sea leaden.

She walks, past the swimming-pool and the miniature golf, past the little café, towards the chimneys of the port.

The stairs.
She climbs the stairs.
She reaches the landing, tries the door.
She opens her bag and feels about in it for the keys.
She sits on the top stair and empties the contents of her bag on to the floor beside her.
She replaces the contents one by one, closes the bag.
She stands up and rings the doorbell.
She waits.

She rings again.

She hammers on the door, first with one hand, then with the other, finally with both.

A door opens on the landing below. Someone comes to the well of the stairs.

She stops banging, listens.

The person who has come to the well of the stairs retreats, a door closes.

She starts to hammer again on the closed door, with both fists, rhythmically.

The door opens.

The man stands in the doorway.

— You locked the door, she says to him.

— Don't you have your keys?

— You locked it.

— I'm sorry, he says.

Sunshine.

The sea.

She walks.

Behind her, the stranger.

She stops. She waits for him to catch up with her.

When he is on a level with her she turns towards him. She says: — What do you want?

— Good afternoon, he says.

— What do you want?

— To talk to you, he says.

She begins to walk again. He walks beside her.

— Always, he says, the sea is different. Every day. Every hour.

— Why are you following me? she asks him.

— I told you, he says. I want to talk to you.

— Why?

— I told you, he says.

– Yes, she says.

They walk. Ahead, the gas-works. In the distance, the chimneys of the port.

– Tell me, she says.

He is silent.

– Tell me, she says.

– You want me to tell you?

– Yes, she says.

– Your hands, he says. Like this. Closed up. Your fists.

He holds his hands out to show her. – In your pockets, he says.

She laughs: – My hands?

– Yes, he says.

She takes her hands out of her pockets and holds them out in front of her.

– I told you, he says.

– Is it so obvious? she asks him.

– It is obvious.

– What business is it of yours how I hold my hands? she asks him.

She walks. He keeps pace by her side.

Finally he says: – If somebody is beating up somebody else on the other side of the street you would pass by and do nothing?

She walks, as she always does, looking at the ground a few feet ahead of her, her hands once more in the pockets of her coat.

– You would pretend not to be there? he says. You would pass by on the other side?

– What are you talking about? she says.

– If you see somebody who is beating himself up on the other side of the street, what would you do?

She starts to laugh again.

– What would you do?

She stops. He stops too. – You feel sorry for me? she asks him.

– No, he says.

– Then leave me alone, she says.
– You don't want to talk to me?
– Leave me, she says. Please.
– As you wish, he says.
He turns. He starts to walk back towards the town. She watches as he goes, but he does not look back.

And again the sea.
She walks.
The tide has been in. Shingle covers the promenade.
She walks slowly, stepping carefully to avoid the larger stones, the deeper puddles.
She walks.
Beside her, the stranger.
– I am quite happy in this town, he says.
– All this concrete? she says. All these benches?
– It is good, the sea, he says.
– You've lived here long? she asks him.
– Some time.
They walk in the direction of the gas-works.
– And before? she says.
– Before?
– Where were you before you came here?
– Many places.
– Like where?
– Many, he says.
– What do you do here? she asks him.
– I walk, he says. Like you.
– No, she says. I mean what job.
– I am looking around, he says. For the moment I am looking around.
– Looking around?
– There are several prospects, he says.
She walks. staring at the ground ahead of her.

– Tell me your name, he says to her.
– My name? she says. Why?
– I do not like to talk to people without knowing their names.
– Why do you talk to me then?
– I explained to you, he says.
She walks. He hurries to keep up with her.
– Still you have not told me your name, he says.
– No, she says.
– I asked you.
– Yes, she says. I heard you.
– You do not wish to tell me?
She walks.
– It does not matter, he says. For the time it does not matter.
– No, she agrees. Then she says: – Flora.
– Flora?
She walks.
– That is your name?
He hurries to keep up with her.
– Flora, he says. I like that name.

Morning.
Fog.
She sits at a table by the window of the health-food café, a cup of coffee in front of her.
The big man is standing beside her.
– You never ask me to sit down any more.
– I find your eating habits repulsive, she says.
He laughs.
He unloads his tray on to the table and squeezes himself in beside her on the little cushioned bench. She draws back to the further end, nearest the window.
– Ts ts ts, he says.
– What does that mean?

He carefully unwraps the first of the little pats of butter. –
You used to be quite fond of me, he says.

– Me?

– You.

She takes a packet of cigarettes out of her bag, selects one,
lights it, returns the packet to her bag.

– One of these days they will ask you to put out your
cigarette, he says.

– Oh? she says.

The lady who serves the coffee comes round the counter
and across the room to them. – I'm sorry, she says. It's
forbidden to smoke in here.

– Who says so? the woman asks her.

She points to a notice on the wall.

– Is that new? the woman asks her.

– No. It's never been allowed. This is a health-food restaurant.

– But I've always smoked in here, the woman says.

– You shouldn't have.

The woman stubs her cigarette out in her saucer. The lady
returns to her counter.

The big man licks his fingers, wipes them on his napkin,
picks up his knife and slits one of his scones in two.

– I even seem to remember a rather passionate embrace, the
big man says.

– What are you talking about? she says.

– You and me, he says.

– You're out of your mind, she says.

– I won't hold you to it, he says.

– You're out of your mind, she says again.

– I was merely reminding you what friends we used to be.

– I have no memory of it, she says.

– Lisa, he says.

– Leave me alone, she says.

– What's come over you? he says.

– Oh for God's sake, she says.

– Lisa, he says. I'm not thinking of myself. I'm thinking of
Alma.

– Alma? she says.

– It upsets me to see you like this, he says. And when I'm upset Alma can't work.

The woman starts to laugh.

– Don't laugh, he says. Her work is important to her.

He bites into the half scone, takes a gulp of coffee to wash it down, sighs, wipes his mouth with the back of his hand.

– I must be nice to you so that you can be nice to Alma so that she can work so that you won't feel guilty? she says. Is that it?

– Lisa, he says. We used to understand each other so well.

She starts to laugh again. He puts the rest of the scone into his mouth and munches steadily, watching her.

– You ridiculous man, she says.

He winks at her.

– What do you want? she says.

– Lisa, he says.

– I shall have to stop coming here, she says. If I want to avoid meeting you.

He slices open the second scone. – Lisa, he says. Be reasonable.

– Why? she says.

He puts a hand on her arm.

– Let me go, she says.

– Lisa, he says. Listen.

– Come on, she says. Let me go. I have things to do.

He stares into her face.

– Come on, she says. I have to go.

– Lisa, he says.

– Will you allow me to get up? she asks him.

– Talk to me Lisa, he says. I'm a good friend.

She pushes away the table and stands up.

– Before you go, he says. Tell me what's happened. What's happened to our friendship?

– Our friendship? she says. What are you talking about?

– Please Lisa, he says. Just this once. Try and see clearly.

– Why? she says.

– Talk to me, he says. You need to talk.
– No I don't, she says. You do. Not me.
– Lisa, he says, how have I failed you?
– Stop it, she says. It isn't funny.
– It isn't meant to be funny Lisa.
He follows her to the door.
– Leave me alone, she says.
In the street he says: – Lisa, just tell me this.
– Go back, she says. Leave me alone.
– Just this, he says.
– You haven't eaten your nut cake, she says.
– It won't run away, he says.
– It might do, she says.
– Lisa, he says, putting a hand on her arm.
She shakes his hand off and hurries away down the street.
He stands, looking after her.
He goes back into the café.

And again, the sea.
She walks.
She walks.

And again, the room.
She says to the man: – A man talked to me. A stranger.
His face is in shadow. He makes no movement.
She crosses the room to the window. She looks out in the
direction of the sea.
She says: – For days he's been following me.
– If you will spend your days walking, he says.
– I thought it would amuse you to hear.
– Amuse me?

She turns back to the room.
– Please, she says.
He is hidden by the high back of the chair.
She says again: – Please.
– I don't understand, he says.
– Yes you do.
– Oh? he says.
She leaves the window and starts to walk round the room.
He waits, watching her.
She sits down on the sofa, facing him.
– I just thought, she says.
– Thought what?
– It might amuse you.
– Amuse me.
– Yes.
– To hear about this man?
– Yes.
– Ah, he says.
She clenches her hands in the pockets of her coat, remembers, unclenches them.

The sea.
She walks.
Above her, the gulls circle and scream.
Ahead, in the distance, the gas-works.
She walks.
She walks.

Sunshine. A strong wind.
She sits with the stranger on a bench in the little park above the cliffs.

Below them the sea is green, creamy. To their right it is
black, with silver stripes.

She says: – Autumn is the best season.

He is silent.

– Here, she says. In England.

– Flora, he says, you must tell me why you walk as you do.

– I like the weather in England, she says. Do you? No two
days are the same. I like that.

– Flora, he says. You must tell me.

– Tell you?

– Why you walk like that.

– What are you talking about? she says.

– It seems to me, he says, that it is a reflection of your inner
condition.

– I don't know how people can bear it, she says. Every day
like every other. In Greece, for example. Or Alaska.

– Why do you talk like that? he says.

– Not that I've ever been to Alaska, she says.

– You do not listen to what I say, he says. I ask you a
question but you do not listen.

She is silent.

The whole sea is dark now. The lines of silver have disappeared.

– You do not answer my question, he says.

– What do you want with me? she says to him. I cannot
understand what you want with me.

– I want to help you, he says.

– But I don't need any help.

– Everybody needs some help, Flora, he says.

– Oh, she says, laughing, that's different.

– I think I can help you, he says.

– You work for some organization? she asks him.

– Pardon?

– A charitable organization? Or a welfare organization?

– I do not understand, he says.

– Dispensing charity, she says. Advice.

– At the moment, he says, I do not have work. I am looking

round. There are various prospects.

– I just wondered, she says.

– Perhaps I will buy a share in an art gallery, he says.

– You're a painter?

– No.

– You know about painting?

– It is not necessary.

She is silent, looking out at the sea.

– I have not yet made up my mind, he says. I think perhaps it is not a good idea. Not in this town.

She leans back and closes her eyes.

– I have been looking round, he says. I have been making enquiries. I feel it is perhaps not right. Not in this town.

She opens her eyes and sees the thin clouds scurrying above her.

– I have to trust my instincts, he says. In the end it is the only thing.

She closes her eyes again.

– In business, he says. In personal affairs. That is the only thing you can trust in the end.

– And your instincts warn you against buying a share in an art gallery, she says.

– In this town, yes, he says.

– So, she says, where is it to be?

– Pardon?

– Where is it to be if not here?

– I do not know, he says. Perhaps I will think of something else. Another kind of thing.

– In another town?

– Perhaps, he says.

– Have you any particular thing in mind?

– Many things, he says.

– And the place?

– Perhaps another country. I will see.

– Oh?

– It does not matter, he says. Where does not matter. There will be a place that will be right. My instinct will tell me. And even if I do not find such a place it does not matter.

– Nothing matters?

– No no, he says. Only for me. For me everything is all right.

– Wonderful, she says.

– Pardon?

– Wonderful I said.

– You see Flora, he says, it is only a matter of instinct. I have learnt that in my life.

And again the stairs.

The room.

She stands, with her back to the door, surveying the room.

She crosses to the bedroom, opens the door, stops.

She stands, looking into the room.

She walks slowly forward and stands again, looking down at the bed.

She lets herself sink slowly down on to it.

She lies, stretched out straight, along the edge of the bed.

Her eyes are open. She is looking up at the ceiling.

The sea.

She walks.

Her hands deep in the pockets of her coat. Her fists clenched tight inside the pockets.

She walks.

She walks.

The empty room.

She leans against the door.

She walks forward into the room and lets herself sink down on to the carpet.

She lies on her back, on the carpet, eyes open, looking up at the ceiling.

Morning. Sunshine.

A windless day.

She sits on one of the benches in the little park, facing the sea. Beside her, the stranger.

He says: – Flora, I would like very much to meet your husband.

– What a funny idea, she says.

– Yes, he says, I would like to meet that man.

– Why?

– I would like.

She asks him suddenly: – Where do you come from?

– Before, he says, I was in Leeds.

– No, she says. I mean before that.

– I was in Leeds two years.

– But before.

– In Edinburgh one year.

She is silent.

– You see, he says, I am interested in what you have told me about your husband.

– I haven't told you anything about him.

– Yes Flora, he says. You have told me.

– What? she says. What have I told you?

– Many things.

– Rubbish, she says.

– I would like to see too what kind of people are your friends, he says.

– I have no friends.

– Excuse me Flora, he says, but you described to me your friends.

– I did?

– Yes.

– Oh, she says. They aren't friends.

– Pardon?

– They're not friends.

– No?

– I may have talked to you about Bertie and Alma, she says. He is my husband's brother. He is a lawyer. Very fat. She makes very bad sculpture. Out of the things she finds on the beach. Stuck together with cement. Faces. Figures.

– It is bad?

– Atrocious, she says.

– Ah, he says.

– He thinks because he's my brother-in-law he more or less owns me, she says.

– Pardon?

– Also a daughter, she says. Fat. Like him. A mathematician.

He is silent, staring down at the sea.

– I don't know why I tell you all this, she says.

– It is good to talk, he says.

– Have you ever heard of a fat mathematician? she asks him.

– Pardon?

– Mathematicians shouldn't be fat, she says. They should be lean.

– I do not understand exactly, he says.

– Never mind.

– Perhaps you can arrange, he says.

– Arrange what?

– That I should meet them.

– Why?

– I should like.

– What are you talking about? she says.

– You see, he says, I have not many friends in this town.

– Too bad, she says.

He takes a notebook out of the pocket of his jacket, pulls a pencil out of its spine, puts the notebook on his knee and starts to write.

He tears out the sheet on which he has been writing and hands it to her.

– What is it?

– I have written my name and address, he says. My temporary address. Soon I will move.

He holds it out to her. She makes no attempt to take it.

– Here, he says. For you.

A mist is rising from the sea which is barely visible now.

– There is a telephone, he says. But my landlady does not like it to be used. So I do not put it down.

She has laid her head on the curved back of the bench and is looking up into the sky again.

– I may phone myself if it is an emergency, he says. But she does not like people to phone me in the house. It is difficult.

– You should move, she says.

– Yes yes, he says. Soon I will move.

She has closed her eyes.

– Here, he says. Take.

He pushes the sheet of paper into her hand but it falls out and flutters to the ground. He bends and picks it up, puts it into her hand again.

– Take, he says. In case of emergency. It is always good to have.

– What emergency? she says. What are you talking about?

– It is better to have, he says.

– I don't want it, she says.

It flutters to the ground again. This time he does not pick it up.

– You will not take it? he asks her.

– It has nothing to do with me, she says. Nothing. Do you understand?

The sea.

She stands, holding on to the railings, her eyes closed.

The sun on her face.
The water lapping against the shingle.
She opens her eyes.
The sea.

The room.
She says: – You hold it against me that I went away?
He shrugs.
– Speak to me, she says.
– What do you want me to say?
– You won't speak to me? she says.
– Yes, he says. Of course I'll speak to you.
– I want to know if you hold it against me, she says.
His face is in shadow.
– Hold what against you? he says.
– That I went away.
He shrugs.
– You won't tell me?
He is silent.
– You can't? she asks him.
– No, he says.
– Why?
– I don't know, he says.
– Not if I help you? she says.
He shakes his head. – No, he says.
– I see, she says. I see.

And again she is walking.
The wind blows into her face.
She walks.
She walks.

The stranger.

– Flora, he says. You have arranged a meeting with your husband?

– No, she says.

– I am curious about that man, he says.

– Why?

– I am curious.

– I have told him all about you, she says. I have warned him that you are probably slightly mad.

– That is all right Flora, he says. You are slightly maddened too and no one will pay any attention to what you will say.

She starts to laugh.

– It is true, he says.

– It is?

– You know Flora, he says, that I am only concerned about you.

– Oh my, she says.

– When I see someone who is walking as you are walking, he says, I would not be a human being if I did not try to do something.

– Like what? she says.

– Pardon?

– Do something like what?

– I have lived in many countries, he says. I have seen many things. I know when I have to trust my instincts.

– What places? she asks him.

– Pardon?

– What places have you lived in?

– Many, he says.

– Tell me.

– Yes, he says. I will tell you.

She stops. She looks at the sea.

– Why end up here? she says.

– It is good, he says. It is good to walk by the sea.

– You like it then.

– Yes, he says. Soon I will go.

– Even though you like it?

– Perhaps you will come with me, he says.

– Me?

– I think it is not good for you to stay here.

– You surprise me, she says.

– It is not really a surprising thing Flora, he says. Anyone can see that it is not good for you here. Anyone can see that in a little while you will burst out.

– Burst out?

– Anyone can see.

– Well well, she says.

– Perhaps you will come with me, he says.

– But why? she asks him.

– Why?

– Why with you?

– Why not?

– And my husband that you want so much to meet? she says. My friends so-called? You think I should leave them behind for ever?

– It is better.

– And your meeting with my husband?

– We will meet, he says. You will introduce us. We will talk.

– About me?

– We will talk.

– You know, she says, he's not a very talkative person.

– Pardon?

– Talking isn't his strong point, she says.

– There is time, he says. I will not leave yet for a little while.

And again the sea.

She walks.

The wind presses her coat against her legs. She keeps her hands in her pockets and walks without taking her eyes off the ground.

Behind her, the town.

She walks past the swimming-pool, past the café, past the villas in their gardens. She walks towards the chimneys of the port.

She walks.

She walks.

And again the sea.

She grips the railings. The surface is rough under her hands where the paint has peeled off.

The tide is out. Gulls strut on the wet patches of sand and chalk below the shingle.

She closes her eyes.

The interior of the town.

Incessant traffic.

She enters a café.

She has not been here before.

She finds a table and sits down.

The waitress moves slowly down the room towards her, aligning bottles of ketchup on the tables as she goes.

She reaches the woman's table and stops.

– Tea, please, the woman says.

– Sugar?

– Yes.

The waitress turns and moves back up the room.

The machine at the counter bursts into life.

The waitress comes back towards her with a cup. She sets it down and tea slops into the saucer.

– Have you got the time please? the woman asks.

The waitress turns and moves back up the room.

The woman takes a cigarette out of her bag and lights it.

The waitress returns.
— Half past, she says.
— Past what?
— Half past, the waitress says again.
— Yes, the woman says. Past what?
The waitress goes away again.
The woman looks round for an ashtray, sees one on an adjoining table, half-rises, takes it, sits again.
The waitress returns. She stands by the table. She says: — Three.
— Thank you, the woman says.
The waitress goes away again. As she moves up the room she straightens the chairs at the empty tables.
The woman looks round. The walls are painted green. The windows are steamed up. In the middle of the wall opposite her there is a clock. The fingers point at twenty-three minutes to four.
The woman watches it, waiting for the minute hand to jerk forward.

She sits with the stranger in the little park above the cliffs.
He says: — Flora, believe me, there is no future for you in this town.
She starts to laugh.
He says: — Why are you laughing, Flora?
— Future, she says. What a word.
— I do not understand, he says.
She is silent, looking out at the sea below them.
— It is important to change sometimes, he says.
— But if everywhere is the same?
— No no, he says.
— You told me so yourself.
— You speak like that because you are still here, he says.
— But you did. One place is as good as another.

– You did not understand me Flora, he says. I said that I can live in one place or another. For me it does not matter. But there is a time when it is good to change.

– If I went to Timbuctoo tomorrow, she says, I would still not be able to sleep.

– You do not sleep?

– No.

– There are good sleeping tablets, he says. They do not harm you and they let you sleep.

– Is that so? she says.

– I worked once in a chemistry shop, he says. I know about these things. Now the sleeping pills are very good.

– What haven't you done? she asks him.

– Pardon?

– Forget it.

He says: – Flora, when I have settled my business perhaps you will come with me.

– It will take long, this business, to settle? she asks him.

– No.

– How long?

– Perhaps a few weeks. Perhaps a few days.

– Isn't that too long to be on sleeping pills? she says. I don't want to get addicted.

– No, he says. It is not too long. There is no addiction.

– You amaze me, she says.

– Pardon?

– I said you amaze me.

– You see Flora, he says, you are bitter because you are still here. When you will have gone from here it will be simple. All your bitterness will go.

– Ah, she says. You're a travel agent, is that it?

– No no, he says. That is a terrible job, a travel agent. Absolutely terrible.

– I thought it might be rather fun.

– No Flora, he says. Believe me. It is a terrible job.

– You speak from experience, she says.

– Believe me, he says. A terrible job. Terrible.

In the Fertile Land

And again the sea.
She stops.
She puts her head back and looks up at the sky.
She shakes her head and starts to walk again.
She walks.
She walks.

A supermarket.
Old women and children push their trolleys against her without apology.
She stands, staring at the packets on the shelves.
Someone says: – You don't speak to me any more?
She turns.
The dark woman says again: – You don't speak to me any more?
– I didn't see you.
– I've been standing in front of you for an hour.
– I'm sorry, the woman says.
– Let's get out of this, the dark woman says. Come and have some iced coffee.
– I don't know if I have time, the woman says.
– Of course you have time, the dark woman says. I've got the car. We'll be home in no time.
– I don't know, the woman says.
– Of course you do, the dark woman says. I could do with some iced coffee, I really could.

In the garden, under the parasol, the dark woman says: – It's terrible. I never see you these days.
– You're so busy, the woman says.
– I am rather, the dark woman says. But it's you I'm

thinking of.
– Me?
– I feel you're trying to avoid me.
– Me?
– I have that feeling.

The woman picks up her glass and drinks. She puts the glass down on the garden table.

The dark woman is looking towards the house.

– How's your work going? the woman asks her.

– You're not interested in my work, the dark woman says. Why should you be? It's rubbish anyway.

The woman picks up her glass again and drinks.

– It was never any good, the dark woman says. And it's getting worse.

The woman leans forward and helps herself to more coffee from the jug.

– I wanted to talk to you, the dark woman says.

– Me?

– About Robert.

– Robert?

– Listen, the dark woman says. I understand how you feel. Believe me. But there are ways of coping with these things.

– Are there? she asks.

– Oh for godsake, the dark woman says.

The woman takes a long drink and puts down the glass.

The dark woman sighs. Then she says:

> Where is that summer, warm enough to walk
> Among the lascivious poisons, clear of them,
> And in what covert may we, naked, be
> Beyond the knowledge of nakedness, as part
> Of reality, beyond the knowledge of what
> Is real, part of a land beyond the mind?

The woman waits.

– Do you know the answer? the dark woman asks her.

– No, the woman says.

– Nowhere, the dark woman says. The answer is nowhere.

– You mean there is no land beyond the mind?

– No, the dark woman says. No summer, no covert, no land.

– You asked me here to tell me that? the woman asks her.

– Yes, the dark woman says.

– I see, the woman says.

– No land, the dark woman says. Don't forget that, Lisa. However far you walk. There is none and there never will be.

The woman stands up.

– You don't have to go yet, the dark woman says.

– Yes, the woman says.

– Lisa, the dark woman says.

– What?

– Be good to him.

– Him? the woman says. Which him?

The dark woman laughs. – Of course, she says. Both. But I meant Robert.

The woman turns away.

– You won't forget? the dark woman asks her.

– Forget?

– No summer. No covert. No land.

The woman starts to walk towards the house. Half way across the lawn she stops and turns. The dark woman is still sitting at the table under the parasol with the jug of iced coffee in front of her. She smiles and waves, shielding her eyes with one hand.

The woman turns away and goes on towards the house, the street, the town, the sea.

The sea.
Again she walks.
Above her float the gulls, screaming.
To her right, the grand hotels.
She walks.

She climbs the stairs.
She enters the room.
She stands in the middle of the room.
She begins to walk round the room.
With the tips of her fingers she touches the walls, the backs of the chairs, the spines of the books on the shelves.
She stands at the window, looking out.
Once more she moves round the room, lightly touching the walls, the tables, the back of the big armchair in the window, the spines of the books.
She stands at the window, looking down into the communal gardens below and, beyond them, at the sea.

Sunshine.
She stands, leaning against the railings, her eyes shut, facing the sea.
She rocks back on her heels, clasping the railings.
The sun on her face.
The tide, sucking at the shingle.

She sits on the bench in the small park above the cliffs.
Beside her, the stranger.
Lines of silver across the black sea.
She says: – The sea wall at Roscoff is immense. You can walk along it and out over the sea on great bridges. Everyone in Roscoff, she says, eats great quantities of seafood. There is nothing but the continuous cracking of bones in the restaurants. And then the sucking in of the flesh. The noise, she says, is deafening.
– I have been to Roscoff, he says.
– One day, she says, I went for a walk. I walked out of the

town and along the cliffs. There was a waiter from the hotel following me. I thought, she says, that if I could get far enough away, where no one knew where I was, I could be myself. Do you understand?

– It is good, he says.

– I was suddenly frightened, she says. Frightened of dying without having understood anything. Anything at all.

He is silent, looking out at the sea.

– Perhaps, she says, I did not go far enough away. Perhaps I should have gone all the way to Finisterre.

– This man, he says. The waiter. He only followed you? He did not approach you?

– I walked right through the afternoon, she says. I walked out of the town along the cliffs. Whenever I turned he was there. Then I would walk some more and forget him, and then remember him again and turn round and he would be there.

– It is the way you walk, Flora, he says. There is something about the way you walk.

– He made no allusion to the event when he served me later, at the hotel, she says. It made me wonder whether I might not have been wrong.

He waits for her to go on.

– I wasn't wrong, she says. I know it was the same one.

He waits, gazing out at the sea.

– My mind was very clear, during that walk, she says. I saw a great deal I had not seen before. I understood a great deal more than I ever had.

She says: – I said to myself: why be there rather than here? Or here rather than there? I said that to myself again and again.

– So, she says, I came back.

He waits.

He looks at her.

She has closed her eyes.

He says: – He came close to you, this man?

– I don't know why I'm telling you this, she says. I don't even know your name.

– I told you my name, he says. I wrote it.

– I don't know why I'm telling you this, she says.

He says: – It is good for you. It is good to look into the past and not turn to one side.

She laughs.

– Yes, he says. It is good.

– It is good, he says, if there is somebody who will listen.

– Like now, he says. I listen to you.

– You want to help me then? she asks, laughing again.

He looks into her face, puzzled.

– You really and truly want to? she says.

He shakes his head. – I do not understand, Flora, he says.

– I find it funny, she says, that you should be so concerned to help me.

– Why funny?

She says: – I don't need help. I don't need your help or anybody else's.

– Flora, he says. That is wrong. Everybody needs help. Even a little. But everybody needs.

The room.

She stands in the doorway of the kitchen, a glass of water in her hand.

She says: – He has been following me again.

The man says: – You know it has nothing to do with me.

– Yes, she says.

Drilling starts up in the street below.

– I talked to him, she says.

He is holding his hands up to the light, examining his nails.

She goes to the window, pushes it shut. The noise of the drilling decreases.

She turns and crosses the room to the sofa, sits.

The man holds his hands up to the light, first one hand and then the other. He turns them slowly in the light, first close to his face, then at arm's length.

She says: – I would have liked to go to Bayeux. I would have liked to see the embroidery.

– You can go any time, he says.

– Yes, she says.

– I never will now, she says.

– Why not? he says. It's not difficult.

– No, she says. I never will. Not now.

Despite the closed window the noise of the drill invades the room.

– It's very simple, he says. No problem at all.

He rubs the knuckles of his left hand gently with the fingers of his right.

– We could drive over, he says. If you wanted.

She gets up again and goes to the window. She looks down into the gardens.

She says: – To walk slowly round that room. To see the story unfolding on the walls. It would have been nice.

– We could stop over on the way, he says. We could go on to Mont-Saint-Michel.

– Yes, she says. It would have been nice. By myself. In the middle of that room. In the middle of that battle.

And again the sea.
She walks.
A strong wind blows straight into her face.
She walks, keeping her face down, leaning into the wind.
She walks.
She walks.

Sunshine.
She stands, looking into a shop window.

Behind her, the sea.

Someone is standing beside her.

- Ah, she says. You.

The big man stands close to her.

She waits.

– Well, he says. Well well.

– Well what?

– Lisa, he says.

He takes her arm and guides her across the road. When they reach the railings he lets go her arm.

– Lisa, he says again.

– What?

– I want to ask you, he says. Why can't we be friends?

– Friends?

– Lisa, Lisa, he says sorrowfully.

– Are you following me around? she asks him.

– Me?

– Are you?

– Because I happened to see you with your friend?

– What friend? she asks him.

– Lisa, he says.

– So, she says. You are.

– Are what?

– Following me.

– Lisa, he says. Just think what you're doing. Just give it a little bit of thought.

– Thought? she says.

He sighs.

– Is that what you wanted to say to me? she asks him.

– Have I done anything to you? he says. Tell me if I have.

– You're not funny, she says.

– Oh I can be funnier than that, he says. When I try. I promise you.

She turns and starts to walk along the broad pavement, keeping close to the railings. He hurries after her and takes her arm.

– Leave me alone, she says.

– Lisa, he says. Won't you talk to me?

– Why? she says.

– You did, he says. Once. Do you remember?

– No, she says.

– It's no use saying no, he says. Facts are facts Lisa.

– Stop it, she says.

– Stop what?

– Did Alma tell you we had coffee together? she says.

– Yes, he says.

– Iced coffee.

– Yes, he says. She told me.

– Why do you keep following me around like this? she asks him.

– Lisa, he says. It's a small town. People bump into each other.

– Well? she says.

– Well what?

– What did you want to say?

– I just wanted to talk to you. I didn't want to say anything.

– I thought when people talked they said things.

– Lisa, he says. Why do you make it all so difficult? It never used to be like that.

– In your head, she says.

– No, he says. In reality.

– If you like, she says.

– No, he says. Not if I like. In reality.

– All right, she says.

– Lisa, he says. You're making it difficult for a lot of people. Don't you see that?

There is a lull in the traffic on the promenade. She turns away from him and starts to cross the road.

– Don't you see that? he calls after her. Don't you see that?

Noon.

The little park on top of the cliffs.

She says to the stranger: – There was a man. In Roscoff. In the hotel. We were alone in the lounge. He asked if I would have coffee with him.

The stranger sits beside her, stiffly, looking out at the sea.

– He told me about himself, she says. The way one does. When one doesn't know someone. When one speaks in a foreign language.

Bars of silver stretch across the sea.

– He was a dentist, she says. He was on a visit to his sister.

The man beside her does not seem to have heard.

– Her house was too small, she says. With all the children. And her husband's mother. So he had to stay in a hotel.

The stranger has not moved.

– He told me about his childhood, she says. He showed me photographs. Of himself and his sister. In a garden. In Bayonne.

– I was in Biarritz once, the stranger says.

– There were other photographs too, she says. Of his sister's children. Of his mother and father. Of his wife. Always in gardens. In sunlight in gardens.

– There are many rich people in Biarritz, the stranger says. Many rich people.

She is silent.

He waits for her to continue, but she is silent.

She walks.

Behind her, the town. Ahead, the gas-works. In the far distance, the chimneys of the port.

She walks.

She walks.

She says: – First I took a room in Rouen. In a hotel in the main square. It was night. I drew back the curtains and there was the tower of the cathedral. Right there above me. Practically inside the room. I found it difficult to sleep.

The stranger walks beside her.

– The size of it, she says. The weight.

He walks, silent.

– After the second night, she says, I couldn't bear it. I couldn't sleep for fear it would fall down on top of me.

– It was so silly really, she says. After all, it hadn't fallen in all those years so why should it suddenly do so now? But if you'd slept in that room you'd have understood.

– I decided to move on, she says. I took a train and went to Roscoff. I wanted to stop in Bayeux and see for myself the details of the tapestry but the trains didn't make that feasible.

She stops. The stranger stops too.

He stands, waiting, beside her.

She looks out at the sea and makes a gesture with her hands, reaching out towards it. Then she starts to walk again.

He walks beside her.

– Actually, she says, even missing out Bayeux I had to keep changing. Even from Paris you have to change. But I didn't want to go to Paris. I didn't want to arrive at one of those huge stations. I didn't want to wait around in one of those places. So I went across country from Rouen.

– I had to get a train to Serquigny, she says. And then change at Mézidon. And again at Le Mans. And finally at Morlaix. Serquigny. Mézidon. Le Mans. Morlaix. That was the only way if you wanted to avoid Paris. From Rouen.

They walk.

Ahead of them, the gas works.

– The waiters were nice to me, she says. In Roscoff. Not in Rouen. It wasn't that sort of hotel. But in Roscoff.

– The lounge was very dark, she says. Full of big leather armchairs. But outside the sun was always shining. Through the door of the lounge, she says, you could see the water sparkling in the sun.

– I walked along the cliffs, she says. And I looked north towards the Cornish coast.

– Cornish? the stranger says.

– Suddenly there didn't seem to be any point, she says. At least I couldn't think of any. Why I was there, I mean.

– Cornish? the stranger says again.

– So I came back, she says.

The stairs.
She climbs the stairs.

The bedroom.
Her coat on the bed.
She stands by the bed, looking down.

She says: – The waiter. The one who followed me. He reminds me of you.

– Yes, the stranger says. I was a waiter once. When I was a student. For one whole summer.

They sit on the bench in the little park on top of the cliffs.

– Where? she asks.

– Where?

– Where was that?

– Pardon?

– Where were you a waiter?

– In Sweden. On a small island.

– You do get around, she says.

– You see Flora, he says, my people are always moving.

– What people is that?

– The Jewish people.

– Oh God, she says.

– That is what history has made us do, he says.

– How can you talk like that? she says.

– Like what, Flora?

– My people, she says. Made us do.

– We are a people, he says. We cannot change it.

– There are only people, she says. Not peoples.

– I did not say peoples.

– I mean, she says, there are only people. Not a people.

– I do not understand.

She closes her eyes.

– My English is not good, he says.

– It's not your English, she says.

He says again: – I do not understand.

– No?

– You do not belong, he says. You cannot comprehend.

– Oh my, she says.

– I will explain to you, he says.

– No, she says. Please.

– You do not want me to explain?

– No.

– Flora, he says. What is needed is that you should talk. That you should not close your hands into fists.

She is staring out at the sea.

– Flora, he says. You cannot stay here. With these people.

– I can do what I like, she says.

– Yes, he says. But it is not what you like.

– How do you know?

– I know, he says.

– I can do what I like, she says again.

– You cannot stay here, he says.

– Where do you suggest I go?

– It does not matter, he says. It is just a question of changing.

– That's all?

– If you come with me Flora, he says, you will see. You will not be able to understand why you stayed so long.

– You have a very great faith in yourself, she says.

– No, he says. In change.

– In change then.

– Well, he says, it is my life.

– You've changed so much? she asks, laughing.

– Always, he says.

She looks out at the sea. – Tell me, she says.

– It is of no interest, he says. Except to me.

– You told me talking was good.

He is silent.

He says: – Abraham. My ancestor. He was told to change and he changed.

– Who told him?

– God, he says.

– Oh, she says. God. That's different, isn't it?

– Even his name was changed, he says.

– That's always the way, she says, laughing. I too have been known to change my name.

– He was told to get up and go, he says. And so he did. After him we have always been ready to get up and go.

She waits. She does not appear to have heard.

– Thirty years, he says. I was in one country. Then I thought: It is eating me up alive. Too much politics. Too much anxiety. I did not want it. I wanted to be me, not the citizen of a state. So I left.

She is silent, looking out at the sea.

– When I left I became myself again, he said. And I became a Jew again.

She says: – Are you frightened sometimes?

– Always, he says.

– Always?

– Always.

– How can you go on then? she asks him.

– I have many things to think about, he says. It stops me thinking about the fear.

– Things like what?

– Always there are things, he says.

– Like what?

– You, he says.
She gets up.
He does not move.
She starts off down the path, back towards the town.
She looks back once but he has not moved.

The stairs.
She climbs.
She opens the door.
The empty room.

The sea.
She breaks into a run. Slows to a walk. Then starts to run
again.
On her left, the sea. On her right the villas in their gardens
at the edge of the town.
She runs, then walks, then runs again.

And again the stairs.
She climbs.
The door.
She struggles for breath.
She enters the room.

And now she walks.
The sea.

A light drizzle blows into her face.
She walks. She walks.
Ahead of her, the chimneys of the port.

The café.
She says to the waitress: – With a little milk. Just a little milk.
– White? The waitress asks.
– Khaki.
The girl waits, turning towards the stranger.
– No, he says. I have a complaint in my stomach.
The woman says: – Yes. All right. White.
The waitress scribbles out the bill and leaves it on the table.
– We have not seen the sun for seven days, he says.
– Time to move on, the woman says.
– Yes, he says. Soon I will move.
The waitress puts the cup of coffee down in front of her.
– Look, the woman says, spooning up the froth. Nothing but air.
– You said white, the girl says.
– Look, the woman says. It could be hot milk with air blown in to fill it out. Where's the coffee?
– You want it black? the waitress asks her.
– Can you see any coffee? the woman asks the stranger. Can you see any coffee at all?
She pushes the cup away from her. – Muck, she says.
The waitress turns and walks away.
– Muck, the woman says.
She says: – I don't know why I come here.
– When I leave Flora, the stranger says, I think you will come with me.
– The coffee isn't any better in Cornwall, she says.
– I do not think Cornwall, he says.
She pulls the cup towards her and bends down to take a sip.

– There is no future for you here, Flora, he says.

She straightens, and wipes her lips with a paper napkin she
has taken from the glass on the table between them.

– What does it mean, a future? she says. Except when it's
done with. And then it isn't a future any more.

– Pardon? he says.

– Never mind.

– Flora, he says.

– You should drink some milk, she says. It'll help settle
your stomach.

– No Flora, he says. Believe me. It is better to drink nothing.

– Let nature do its work?

– Believe me, he says. I studied some medicine at one time.
For these things it is better to do nothing.

And again the sea.
She walks.
The murmur of the tide, far away,
A dog barks on the beach below.
She walks.
She walks.

And now she sits in the lounge of the hotel in Roscoff and
says to the man sitting in the armchair opposite: – At this very
moment my husband is returning from a visit to the country.
He has been to see his son.

– Ah yes? the man says.

– He has been to visit his child, she says.

The man signals to a waiter and asks for more coffee.

– You see, she says, I have not given him any children. I
have only taken his child away from him. I have caused the
separation of this man and his child.

– He cannot see the boy? the man asks.

– Once a month, she says. Each time he sees him it is a little worse. Each time he senses that the child is unhappy and he grows more and more unhappy himself.

– The mother turns the boy against him? the man asks.

– No no, she says. Nothing like that. But he sees him so rarely. He feels the boy is drifting away from him. In his heart he blames me.

The uniformed waiter returns with a new jug of coffee on a silver tray.

– Will you? the man asks her.

– Please.

The waiter blocks out the light as he bends over her cup. He fills the other cup and leaves the jug and tray on the low table between them.

– I blame myself, she says.

– It takes time, you know, the man says, dropping a lump of sugar into his cup. Such things always take time to resolve themselves.

– I have given it time, she says. If you only knew the time I have given it.

– We are always in too much of a hurry, the man says.

– Always?

He brings the cup to his lips.

– Always? she asks him again.

– We never give things enough time, he says.

– Where is it to come from? she asks him.

– To come from?

– Time. Where is it to come from?

– Ah, he says. Time. He laughs.

– I have looked everywhere, she says. I have not found it.

– You have not found it? He laughs again, puzzled.

– I have turned my pockets inside out, she says. My bag. My head. I have not found it.

– Well, he says, these things are sometimes hidden from the one who looks too anxiously.

– What does that mean? she asks him.

Roscoff.
The cliffs.
She walks away from the town, looking out across the sea
towards the Cornish coast.
The waves thunder against the rocks below.
She walks. She stops. She walks again.
She walks.
She walks.

In the lounge of the hotel she says to the man: – You see, he
has a son. By a previous marriage. Anthony. Not a name I
would have chosen myself, but there it is.
The man holds down the lid of the silver coffee-pot as he
empties the contents into his cup.
– I would have liked to bear him a child, she says.
– There is time, no? the man says.
– Yes, she says.
The man leans back, crosses his legs, holding his trousers at
the knee so as to maintain the crease – His first wife, he asks,
she is married again?
– Oh yes, she says. Oh yes.
– And she has more children?
– Two.
– And the new husband? He likes the child? Anthony?
– Yes yes, she says. It's nothing like that. Only the un-
happiness of my husband, you understand.
– He has to choose, no? the man says.
– I think he feels he made the wrong choice, she says.
– What is the right choice? the man asks.
– It's what he feels, she says.
– He will change, he says.
– No, she says. It just gets worse.
– Perhaps it must get worse before it gets better, the man
says.

– No, she says. It just gets worse and worse and he says less and less. He does not know what to do any more.

– Who can tell? he says. Human beings have an infinite capacity for adaptation.

– Yes, she says. Perhaps.

The sea.
She walks.
In the pockets of her coat, her clenched fists.
She stops.
She turns.
She looks back at the town.
She starts to walk again, towards the town.
She passes the café, the miniature golf, the swimming-pool.
In the pockets of her coat, her clenched hands.
She walks.
She walks.

The little park on top of the cliffs.

She says to the stranger: – At first I had not noticed that anyone was following me. I was intent only on the cliffs, the sea. Then I looked round and saw him. I thought it was only another walker. It was only later that I realized he was following me.

The stranger is searching in the pockets of his jacket.

She says: – And then all of a sudden I realized that it was the waiter from the hotel.

The stranger has taken the notebook from his pocket. He pulls a pencil from its spine and opens it on his knee.

– Perhaps he was not following me at all, she says. Perhaps he was only walking on the cliffs on his afternoon off. Perhaps he didn't recognize me. He gave no sign of recognition when he served me at table that evening.

The stranger tears the sheet of paper on which he has been writing out of his notebook. – I have written my address, he says. Also my telephone number. My landlady does not like people to telephone but if it is an emergency of course it is all right.

– I wondered, she says, if I went out the next day, if he would follow me again.

– Here, the stranger says. Take.

– What's this? she says.

– I have written my address.

– I don't want it.

– Take, he says.

– Why?

– Flora, he says. You cannot stay here. Anybody can see that you cannot stay here. It is finished between you and your husband. It is better to go away with me.

– Why? she says. Why should I go away with you?

– Only because I am here, he says. Because I can arrange things. That is often what holds back. The fear of the little details of arrangement.

– Oh I'm good at the little details, she says. It's the big details that bother me.

– It is easier if there is somebody else, he says.

– What makes you think I don't already have someone else doing the arranging? she says, smiling up into the sky.

– No Flora, he says. I do not think so.

She rummages in her bag, finds the packet of cigarettes and the lighter, takes them out, selects a cigarette, lights it, returns the packet and the lighter to her bag.

– It is a matter of decision, he says.

She leans back on the bench and closes her eyes. She lets the smoke trickle out through her nostrils and smiles up into the sky.

– It is good to move on, he says. I know.

– For you perhaps, she says.

– For everybody, he says. You know the saying: the worst
thing is to move other people from their homes and the best is
to move yourself.

– Because somebody said that it doesn't mean it's true, she
says.

– Of course, he says. Each must have his view. But you will
see that for you what I have said is right. Take.

– I don't want it, she says.

– Take, he says. You may need.

– I don't need anything, she says.

– We all need, Flora, he says. We all need.

Night.
She walks.
Cars swish past her on fat tires and disappear. She turns her
face towards the sea to avoid the glare of the oncoming headlights.

A wind has risen. The air has grown colder. She clenches
her fists inside the pockets of her coat and hunches up her
shoulders.

She walks.
She walks.

She climbs the stairs.
She enters the room.
She stands inside the room, her back to the door.
The man says: – It's late.
She says: – Yes.
The curtains have not been drawn and the moon lights up
the room. The man is barely visible in the high-backed chair
in front of the window.

He says: – Now you're going to walk all night as well.

She stands, leaning back against the door.

He waits.

He says: – The police will pick you up. They will call me out in the middle of the night to identify you.

– It's a free country, she says.

– Yes, he says. But even so.

She says: – You couldn't sleep?

– Why do you say that?

– I wondered.

– No, he says.

– You couldn't?

– That's right.

– You were waiting for me?

– I couldn't sleep, he says.

She leans against the door and closes her eyes.

She says: – Can't we talk?

– I thought that's what we were doing, he says.

– You know what I mean.

– It's impossible to talk to you when you're in this mood, he says.

She waits.

He is silent.

She says: – I had to do something.

He is silent.

– Don't you see? she says.

He is silent.

It is impossible to tell if he is asleep or waiting for her to continue.

– Don't you? she says again.

– You see, she says to the stranger, at times like that it is easy to talk. Everything is so quiet around you and you have just met a person and suddenly you are talking.

– Flora, he says. Listen to me.

– It's easy to say things in a foreign country, she says. You say things and they sound good as you say them. They even sound true.

– Flora, he says.

– You even believe them yourself while you are saying them, she says.

– As if, she says, in another life they might be true. And for a moment you are actually living that other life. Do you know what I mean?

– Flora, he says.

– As you speak, she says, it starts to make sense. As you speak you start to understand what it was like.

– Flora, he says. One little thing and everything begins to go wrong in a person's life. And one little thing and it goes right.

– So it's nobody's fault? she says.

– What is a fault, Flora? he asks her.

She is silent.

– Afterwards, he says, everybody can find the fault. Each person blames himself. But that is not the truth.

– How simple, she says.

– Many people go through their lives, Flora, he says, and never learn this truth.

– Oh my, she says.

– Yes Flora, he says.

She starts to laugh.

– Why? he says. Why do you laugh?

– Me? she says. Laugh?

– You are laughing, Flora, he says. You are laughing and you will not tell me.

– That's not laughter, she says. Not what I call laughter anyway.

Night.
She picks her way over the stones to the edge of the water.

Rats scurry across the beach behind her.

She reaches the edge of the sea. She bends and dips her hand in the water as a wave eddies around her feet.

She brings her hand to her mouth.

Salt on her tongue.

She turns.

She starts to walk back over the stones to the promenade above.

Behind her the waves tug gently at the stones.

Roscoff. The hotel.

In the lounge, drinking coffee after dinner, she says to the man: — It's always the first Sunday of every month. Unless it's in the middle of the school holidays or something like that. He has to change trains, she says, and then take a taxi from the little country station.

The waiter arrives with their coffee on a silver tray.

— He gets there in time for lunch, she says. He has lunch with his former wife and then he takes the boy out. Sometimes they go to a fair in one of the nearby towns. Sometimes they just take a walk down to the river and then have tea in the village. He has to have him back by six. Earlier in the winter. The taxi is waiting for him. It drives him to the station. He tries to give himself ten minutes at the station before the train arrives. He hates having to rush.

— The boy never comes to stay with you? the man asks.

— Now, she says, they are thinking of shutting down the line. It's uneconomical, you see.

— The wife will not let him come to stay with you? he asks her.

— Sometimes, she says, they go to a film in town.

— You are fond of the boy? the man asks.

— Me?

— Yes.

– I hardly know him, she says. She adds: – I could be fond of him you know.

– He does not stay with you then in his holidays? the man asks.

– No, she says.

– Ah, the man says.

– I could be, she says. It's just that I haven't been given the chance. I haven't been given the chance to get to know him properly.

The sea.

She walks.

Beside her, the stranger.

– Soon I have finished with this town, he says. Now I have to make my plans. Perhaps I will move to Devon. Or to Somerset.

– Why there? she says.

– You know Devon? he asks her. You know Somerset?

– A little.

– You like it?

– Why? she says. Why there?

– Why?

– Yes.

– Because it is finished here, he says. My business is finished.

– What business is that?

– Flora, he says, you will come with me when I go?

She is silent.

– Flora, how many years you have lived in this town? he asks her.

– Four years, she says. Five.

They pass the café. It is closed.

– Since my marriage, she says.

– I feel I will die here, she says.

– No Flora, he says. You must not speak like that.

– Why not?

– It is bad to speak like that.

– I never wanted to live here, she says. I didn't like it. It's a holiday town. It's not real. I miss trees too. But now I feel I will die here. I won't even mind very much, she says.

They walk. Ahead of them, the gas-works. In the distance, the chimneys of the port.

– For you, she says, perhaps there is no place to die.

– No place, any place, he says.

They walk.

– My people have died in every country in the world, he says.

She is suddenly angry. – What do you mean my people? she says. Why do you go on about your people like that? In what way are they yours?

He is silent.

– In what way? she says. In what way?

He gestures with his right hand.

– Go on, she says. Tell me.

– How?

– You said it, she says. Not me.

– You cannot understand, he says.

– That's too easy.

– Why easy?

– Easy to say.

He is silent.

They walk.

He says: – It only makes it easier to move on, he says. When you have tried it you will see.

– I tried, she says.

– Alone it is not so easy.

– You think so?

– I know, he says.

– You know?

– Yes.

– It must be good, she says. To have such confidence. Always to know.

– One does not have, Flora, he says. Always one has to work at it.

She climbs the stairs.

The room.

There is a cigarette crushed out in the ashtray on the little table by the sofa.

She picks up the ashtray and takes it into the kitchen. She opens the dustbin with her foot, empties out the cigarette butt and the ash, lets go the lid, turns on the hot water tap, slowly and carefully washes the ashtray.

She stands at the sink, drying the ashtray.

Night

She lies on the bed.

The bedroom door is open. The flat is empty.

She looks out at the stars through the open window.

Footsteps on the stairs.

The door opens.

The man stands in the main room.

He crosses the room and goes into the kitchen.

He fills the kettle, plugs it in, switches it on.

He crosses to the bedroom. He stands in the doorway.

He says: – Are you unwell?

Her eyes are open. She is looking out at the night sky.

He goes back into the kitchen, takes the teapot from its place in the cupboard, pours a little hot water from the kettle into it to warm it.

The little park above the cliffs.

She says: – At first there was such a feeling of elation. As though at last I had reached my goal.

The stranger is silent.

She says: – Rouen. Getting to Rouen. That was just reflex. I hardly know how I got there. But when I reached Roscoff I felt I had left everything behind me.

— When one is alone one feels a new thing every moment, he says.

— I liked the bridges to the causeway high above the sea, she says. I liked the walks along the cliffs.

— Sometimes, he says, when you think you are very well, that is the beginning of something bad.

— No, she says. It wasn't that. It was just that after that conversation over coffee that evening there was somehow no longer any reason to stay.

— You saw this man again? he asks her.

— No, she says. She adds: — He was visiting his sister.

— The photos that he showed you, he says. Perhaps it was this which made you wish to return.

— There was just no reason to stay, she says.

He spreads out his hands. — There are always too many reasons, he says.

— I don't believe I'll ever move again, she says. I don't believe I will.

He is silent, looking at the backs of his wide-open hands.

— When I stand still I feel dead, she says. I have to be on the move the whole time. I close my eyes and I see myself walking. I open them and I am.

— Yes, he says. It is good to change.

— I'm not talking about change, she says. I'm talking about having to keep moving.

— Yes Flora, he says. I know what you are talking about. It is because you are still here that you talk like this.

— No, she says. I have been elsewhere and I know.

The sea.

She walks down the steps from the promenade to the beach below.

The tide is retreating. At the further edge, close to the water, the stones gleam wetly.

She picks her way carefully to the edge of the water and stops. The tide tugs insistently at the shingle about her feet.

Someone is coming over the beach towards her.

She turns.

The big man walks forward till he is standing almost on her toes.

– You followed me, she says.

He smiles at her.

– You've been following me, she says.

– You have a hyperactive imagination, he says.

– You admit it?

– Relax, he says. Relax.

– Don't you ever do any work? she asks him. What kind of a lawyer are you?

– Not a very good one, I'm afraid, he says.

She has turned away from him and is looking out to sea. The sun shines down out of a cloudless sky.

– I remember a time, he says, when you looked positively glad to see me.

– In your head, she says.

– No Lisa, he says. Not in my head.

– As you like, she says.

– No, he says. Not as I like. As it was.

– If you like, she says.

– Lisa, he says. What have I done to you? Why have you turned against me like that?

– Stop it, she says.

– But I want to know, he says. I have a right to know.

– You're not funny, she says.

– Haven't I? he asks her.

– You tire me, she says. You don't know how you tire me.

– Just this once, he says. Then we can forget it. We needn't ever talk about it again. I think, he says, I deserve an explanation.

– Deserve? she says.

– Lisa, he says.

– Please go, she says. Please. Just go.

He stands close to her, not moving.

She turns away from him quickly and starts to run back over the stones of the beach to the promenade.

– I want an explanation, he calls out after her. That's all. Is it too much to ask?

At the top of the steps she looks back. He stands with his back to the sea, his mouth open, watching her.

The man.

He pads about the flat in his socks.

He flicks a duster over the bookshelves.

He goes into the kitchen and fills the kettle.

He opens a drawer, takes out two spoons, opens a cupboard, takes out two cups and saucers, puts the spoons in the saucers, puts the cups and saucers on a tray, places a bowl of sugar beside them, opens the fridge and takes out a jug of milk, puts it on the tray between the cups. He heats the pot, empties it, puts in the tea. The kettle boils and he fills the pot. He takes one of the spoons off the tray and stirs, then puts the lid back on and places the pot on the tray between the two cups.

He carries the tray into the main room.

He says: – I've made some tea.

The sea.

She walks.

She climbs the path that leads to the little park above the cliffs.

A strong wind blows.

She walks down the alleys of the little park, flicking at the deserted benches with her gloved hands.

The stunted trees.

She sits down in the exact middle of the central bench, looking out over the sea.

The wind.

She stretches her legs out in front of her, keeping her hands deep in the pockets of her coat, staring out at the rough sea.

Time passes.

It grows dark.

She does not move.

The café on the front.

She says to the waitress: — One coffee.

— Black or white?

— It doesn't matter.

The girl looks her over, then tosses the hair out of her eyes, bends over the table and scribbles out a bill.

— It all tastes the same here, the woman says.

The girl appears not to have heard. She turns away and busies herself tidying up a nearby table.

— There are times, the stranger says, when it is even worse when two people know each other than when they do not.

The woman carefully studies her bill.

— They know each other even less than if they did not know each other at all.

— Fifty pence, the woman says. For one cup of air. Can you believe it?

— When I saw you with your husband, he says, I knew it was like that.

— You saw us? she says. Where?

— In the street.

— You spied on us?

— You walked in front of me and you did not see me, he says.

— No, she says. I didn't see you.

The waitress comes back and sets the cup of coffee down in

front of the woman. Some of it spills into the saucer and a
drop lands on the green plastic table-cloth.

– Do you think it would be possible to turn the music down
a little? the woman asks her.

– The music?

– Yes.

– It's for atmosphere.

– I realize that, the woman says. But I wondered whether it
could be turned down a little.

– No, the girl says.

– Ah well, the woman says.

– Will there be anything else? the girl asks, looking at the
stranger.

He waves his hands in the air. – No no.

The waitress goes away.

– You were walking slowly, the stranger says to the woman.
You were not speaking together.

She picks up the cup and pours the spilt coffee back into it
from the saucer.

– It is not good, he says.

– It's all right, she says. If you don't expect too much.

– No, he says. I mean to walk like that.

She laughs.

He leans towards her. She draws back in her seat.

– Don't be afraid, he says. I won't touch you.

She takes a cigarette from her bag and lights it.

He says: – Sometimes it happens like that.

– Does it?

– Yes Flora, he says. I know.

– Why do you think you know everything? she asks him.

– No, he says. I do not know everything. Only some
things. Some things, yes.

The cigarette has gone out. She digs about in the bag, finds
the lighter again, relights the cigarette, drops the lighter back
in the bag.

– I can see what is in front of my face, he says.

She is looking out of the window at the sea. The glass is

streaked and dirty.

– Yesterday, he says, I finalized my plans.

– Finalized? she says.

– Yes.

– Did you say you'd lived in America? she asks him.

– No no Flora, he says. I have never wanted to go to that place.

– I just thought, she says.

– No no, he says. I have never been.

She stubs out her cigarette and gets up abruptly.

– You are going now Flora? he asks her.

– Yes, she says.

She reaches for the bill but he covers it with his hand. She shrugs, turns away from the table, makes for the door.

He watches her, his hand still on the bill, as she pushes open the door and steps out into the wind.

Night.

She walks.

The road leaves the sea and runs past enormous, brightly-lit gas containers.

She walks fast, looking straight ahead of her. The wind drives into her face.

Cars swish past her on fat wheels, throwing mud up in her direction.

She walks, blinking in the face of the headlights of the oncoming cars.

Day.

Sunshine. The air is quite still.

She walks.

On her left, the sea.
Ahead, the chimneys of the port.
She walks.
She walks.

The stranger says: – Now you must be ready. Next Sunday
you must be ready.

She looks down at the sea spread out beneath her.

– Next Sunday, he says. I have the tickets. I have the
bookings.

– You're leaving? she asks him. For good?

– I have told you, he says. You do not listen. I have told you
already.

– Where are you planning to go? she asks him.

– Leave it to me, he says.

– Leave what?

– I have told you Flora, he says. But you do not listen.

She closes her eyes. The sun on her face.

– You will see, he says. You will see that everything will
now change.

She starts to laugh.

– Why? he says. Why do you laugh, Flora?

She cannot stop.

– Why? he says. Tell me why you are laughing. What have
I said that has made you laugh?

She cannot stop. Her body shakes.

– Tell me, he says. You must explain to me.

Finally she is quiet again.

– You must, he says.

– Why? she says. Why must I do anything for you?

– It does not matter, he says. One day I will understand why
you laugh.

She gets up. He follows. She starts to walk away, quickens
her pace.

She runs down the path and out of the little park with its stunted trees and broken-down benches.

She leaves him behind.

The stairs.

She enters the room.

The window behind the armchair is open to the night sky but the room is in darkness.

She sits on the sofa.

She says: – What is it?

Someone shouts in the gardens below.

She says: – You know, I won't be able to bear this much longer.

She strains to see his face but all that is visible is the outline of the high-backed chair.

She says: – How much longer will this go on for?

It seems to her that he is smiling.

She says: – If you want me to call a doctor?

Someone starts to sing drunkenly in the gardens below.

She waits.

She gets up and goes past him, to the window.

She stares down into the gardens and then out at the sea beyond, white under the moon.

She turns back to the room.

– Please, she says.

She stands behind his chair.

– Please, she says again.

Another drunk has joined in the song.

– I beg you, she says.

Night.

Drizzle.

She pushes her hands deep into the pockets of her coat, fists clenched, her shoulders hunched against the wind and rain.

She walks under the giant chimneys of the port.

Cars swish past in an unending stream. The rain blows into her face.

She walks.

A steamer hoots in the lagoon.

She walks.

She walks.

– Tomorrow, the stranger says. Tomorrow you will meet me at the station at the time I have written here.

– Why? she says.

– I have written the time and the platform, he says.

He puts a piece of paper into her hand. She lets it fall to the floor.

He retrieves it, smoothes it out on the table and reads: – Eleven forty-seven. Platform three.

He folds the piece of paper and pushes it into the pocket of her coat.

– When you are in the train with me you will understand how simple it is, he says.

She is not looking at him. She is looking past him, out of the window, over the sea.

– There is nothing to regret, he says. There is never anything to regret, you know.

– Regret? she says.

– No.

He gets up. – I must do many things, he says. I will meet you at the station tomorrow.

She looks past him, through the rain-spattered window, at the grey sea.

She stands, leaning against the railings, her eyes closed, the sun on her face.

The waves tug at the stones, pull them away from the beach, return to tug again.

She rocks gently on her heels, holding on to the railings, her face turned up to the sun.

She walks.

On her left, the chimneys of the port. On her right, the railway line.

She enters a café.

She sits.

A waitress approaches. She says: – Tea, please.

It is hot in the café, airless. She gets up to take off her coat and finds herself at the door. She pushes it open and steps outside.

She stands on the pavement, breathing deeply.

She starts to walk again.

She walks.

The road narrows.

She keeps close to the walls of the houses, but even so the cars almost touch her as they swish past in the dark. Occasionally they hoot as they approach her and she jumps and presses herself against the wall, waiting for them to go by.

When cars come rushing towards her, their headlights on, she stops and puts her hands up to protect her face. When they are past she resumes her walk.

In the lounge of the hotel in Roscoff she says to the man: – When I walk I feel I'm alive. When I sit here, with you, or by myself, I lose any sense of myself. I am not sure if I have already been here before or even if I am really here now. At least when I walk, she says, I know I am walking. I know something is happening, the wind blowing in my face is this wind blowing in my face now, the patterns the sun and clouds throw on the water are these patterns and no others.

She leans forward in the cool dark room and touches the silver coffee-pot with her finger. – This man, she says. This big man. My brother-in-law. I could never tell if he was serious or if he was joking. You know the way some Englishmen are. They say something jokingly when they are serious and seriously when they are joking. I don't think he knew himself half the time which of the two it was, she says.

– Yes, the man says. I have met such Englishmen.

– I have always been afraid of him, she says. Ever since I first met him. I don't know what he wants. Wherever I went, she says, I saw him. Whenever I sat down he was there, standing by my chair. Whenever I went down to the beach he was there, following me. I don't know what he wanted.

– You are sure of this? the man asks. You could not speak to your husband about it?

– His wife, she says, makes sculpture out of stones she picks up on the beach. She builds them up into faces and mounts them on concrete.

– She is a good artist? the man asks.

– Atrocious, she says.

– Ah, the man says.

– There was another man, she says. First he followed me and then he talked to me and finally he wanted me to go away with him. I did not know what to say to him.

The man says: – There are many strange people in the world.

– He showed me tickets, she says. He wrote the time and the platform on a little piece of paper. I did not know what he wanted.

The man is silent. She too seems to have forgotten his presence.

Through the open doorway of the lounge the sea glitters in the bay.

The man says: – As a dentist I see many strange people.

She looks up at him: – You're a dentist?

He nods: – Yes.

She says: – But aren't all mouths the same?

He laughs. He calls the waiter. He points to the pot and asks for more coffee.

– There was a little park, she says. On the cliffs above the town. No one comes to that park. There's too much wind. This man sat there with me, day after day. He told me he had plans. I found I could talk to him easily. He didn't really listen. His plans filled his head.

– Sometimes, the man says, it is easier like that.

She says: – I could not stay any longer. I could not stay and talk to him. I don't know why I am saying this to you.

– As a dentist, the man says, it is necessary to be very intimate with people. And also very distant. You put your fingers inside their mouths, what could be more intimate than that? And then you make them pay. What could be more impersonal?

– I never thought of it like that, she says.

– When you are tired, he says, you do not see people. Even when you meet them socially. At a dinner. At a party. You see teeth. Only teeth.

– What made you become a dentist then? she asks him.

– I have often asked myself that question, he says. And I have never been able to answer it.

She laughs.

– Think of it, he says. Something that you do for more hours of your life than you do anything else and you don't even know why you embarked on it in the first place.

– Perhaps there was a reason, she says. But you've never troubled to unearth it.

– Yes, he admits, laughing. Perhaps there was a reason. Who knows?

Night.

Drizzle.

The giant chimneys of the port.

She walks.

She leaves the port behind her.

Cars swish by on fat tires, throwing her shadow up onto the wall beside her.

Now she no longer stops when cars come towards her, their headlights glaring. She narrows her eyes but keeps on walking.

She walks.

She walks.

The room.

The big man says: – Why, after all, should we expect other people to behave as we would?

– After all, he says, there are billions of people in the world, each one born into particular circumstances and moulded by particular events. Why should we always feel surprise when they act in ways we don't expect?

– And yet, he says, we do.

The dark-haired woman murmurs: – Where is that summer, warm enough to walk?

There is a ring at the doorbell. The man looks at the others, then gets up from his armchair by the window and goes to the door.

He opens it.

The stranger is standing on the landing, a suitcase on the floor beside him.

The man holds the door ajar. He says: – Yes?

– Flora? the stranger says.

– Wrong address, the man says. He closes the door.

The bell rings again at once. The man opens it.

– Robert? the stranger asks.

– Yes, the man says.

– Flora?

– Sorry, the man says. He tries to close the door again but the stranger holds it open.

– She did not meet me at the station, the stranger says.

– I'm sorry, the man says. There's no Flora here.

The big man comes to the door, glass in hand. – Wait a minute, he says.

The stranger looks from one to the other.

– You're Jacob? the big man asks.

– You know me?

– Come in, come in, the big man says. What a surprise.

The two men inside the room step back. The stranger follows them, carrying his large suitcase. He stands in the middle of the room.

– Meet my wife, the big man says. Jacob. Alma.

– She did not meet me, the stranger says.

– We were just talking about her, the big man says.

The stranger looks round the room.

– She's not here, the big man says.

– Flora?

– We call her Lisa.

– Pardon?

– Lisa, the big man says. That's her name.

– She told me Flora, the stranger says.

He stands, looking from one to the other, the suitcase at his feet.

– Here, the big man says. Have a drink.

The stranger does not move.

– Here, the big man says, thrusting a glass into his hand. Cheers.

– She told me this address, the stranger says.

– She did? the big man says. She asked you round? Good show. Delighted. I'm not your host of course. Robert here is. But delighted all the same.

The stranger stands in the middle of the room, glass in hand.

– She's not here, the big man says. Sorry. Vanished. Like

that. Phutt.

– She said she would meet me at the station, the stranger says. He makes a quick movement and puts the glass down on a little table by the sofa.

– Seeing you off, was she? the big man asks.

– She was leaving with me, the stranger says.

The big man whistles. The dark-haired woman says:

– With you?

The big man laughs. – She's an independent girl, Lisa, he says. Likes to go her own way.

The man is sitting again in the chair by the window. His face is lost in shadow. He is looking at his hands.

The dark-haired woman says: – She was to meet you at the station? You were to leave together?

– I have the tickets, the stranger says.

– Well, the big man says, she's not here and she's not there. So where is she?

– She said, the stranger says. He looks down at his bulging suitcase.

– So you didn't take the train? the woman says. You came here to find her?

The stranger looks at her. – You know where she is? he asks her.

– She's not been seen for twenty-four hours, the woman says. We thought you might have news of her.

– I?

– Why not?

– She said she would come, the stranger says.

The woman gets up and offers him a bowl of nuts. He shakes his head. – Thank you, he says.

– You might as well make yourself comfortable, the big man says. We may have a long wait.

– She will come back here? the stranger asks.

– Who knows? the big man says.

The stranger looks across at the man sitting by the window. – She will come back? he asks him.

The man looks up, gazes at him.

– Will she?

– I don't know, the man says.

– Sooner or later, the big man says. Sooner or later. No doubt about it. We'll have her back.

– She said Flora, the stranger says. I asked her and she said Flora.

– You mustn't pay too much attention to what she says, the big man says.

The dark-haired woman gets up again, takes hold of the suitcase and drags it to the side of the room. She pulls up a chair for the stranger to sit down.

He sits.

– Is there something else we could offer you? the big man asks him. Orange juice? Tomato juice? Grapefruit juice? Water?

The stranger is looking at the man sitting in the chair by the window.

– He had his ticket, the dark-haired woman says.

– But he didn't use it, the big man says.

– He had his chance, she says.

– But he threw it away, he says.

– He came to find us, she says.

– He came to seek her, he says.

– That was his journey, she says.

– That was his journey.

The stranger says to the man: – She will not come back.

The man says: – You think so?

– She will not, the stranger says.

The man makes a little gesture with his hands.

– It is better, the stranger says.

– You think it is better?

The dark-haired woman says: – She wants to go. She wants to empty her head of us. But it cannot be done. There is no such summer.

The stranger says: – Pardon?

– At this very moment, she says, she is seeing this room in her head. She is seeing the four of us like this. She tries to escape but it can't be done.

The stranger says: – She said Flora. I asked her and she said Flora.

The dark-haired woman says: – She will not forget. She will hear your voice in her head. She will see your face. Again she will walk by the sea. Again she will speak to me. Again she will hear me say to her: There is no such summer. She will see me stand in this room and she will hear me say: There is no such summer.

The man is looking down at his hands. His face is in shadow.

In the garden below a girl starts to laugh.

The man says suddenly to the stranger: – You play chess?

The stranger turns towards him. – Yes, he says. I play.

– We must play then, the man says. If you're staying, that is.

– I would like, the stranger says.

– So would I, the man says. I have been starved of opponents for too long.

– Did you hear that? the big man says. He has been starved of opponents for too long.

– And me, the stranger says. I have also been starved of opponents.

– I can't believe it, the big man says. I honestly can't believe it. They have both been starved of opponents. Can you believe it? They have both been starved of opponents, and for too long.

But his wife does not answer. She is looking at the door.

MORE CARCANET FICTION

Sebastian Barry   *The Engine of Owl-Light*
'He must be regarded as one of the most promising of our writers, displaying a technical ambition and an emotional maturity . . .'
                                                           IRISH TIMES

Emmanuel Bove   *Armand*
'. . . does for Paris what Ulysses did for Dublin.'   THE NEW YORKER

Christine Brooke-Rose   *Xorandor*
'. . . verbal pyrotechnics are deployed in the interest of heightening and enriching her story, which is always riveting.'
                                          NEW YORK TIMES BOOK REVIEW

Dino Buzzati   *The Tartar Steppe*
'It is not often a masterpiece falls into one's hand . . . *The Tartar Steppe* is a sublime book and Buzzati a master of the written word.'   SUNDAY TIMES

Stuart Hood   *A Storm from Paradise*
'. . . its passionate artistic truth is conveyed in writing so plain, realistic and indeed functionally beautiful that one learns its sad lessons from history with joy.'   FINANCIAL TIMES

Clarice Lispector   *The Hour of the Star*
'The literary discovery of the decade'   VOGUE

Pier Paolo Pasolini   *A Violent Life* and *The Ragazzi*
'. . . both are extraordinary. Written in the 1950s, they are energetic, blithely amoral accounts of life in the suburban slums of Rome, seen largely through the eyes of their more or less criminal inhabitants.'   THE LISTENER

Umberto Saba   *Ernesto*
'This little gem is the last testament of one of Italy's most revered modern poets. A lovely, classical portrait of adolescence.'
                                                      BOOKLIST (ALA)

Leonardo Sciascia   *Sicilian Uncles* and *One Way or Another*
'What is the Mafia mentality? What is the Mafia? What is Sicily? When it comes to the exploration of this particular hell, Leonardo Sciascia is the perfect Virgil.'   GORE VIDAL

Michael Westlake   *Imaginary Women*
A novel to be read as geopolitics, as postmodernism, as homage to Hollywood, as psychoanalysis, as anarchic fiction . . .